SAMSKARA
A Rite for a Dead Man

Sam-s-kāra. 1. Forming well or thoroughly, making perfect, perfecting; finishing, refining, refinement, accomplishment. 2. Forming in the mind, conception, idea, notion; the power of memory, faculty of recollection, *the realizing of past perceptions* . . . 3. Preparation, making ready, preparation of food, etc., cooking, dressing . . . 4 . . . 5. Making sacred, hallowing, consecration, dedication; consecration of a king, etc. 6. Making pure, purification, purity. 7. A sanctifying or purificatory rite or essential ceremony (enjoined on all the first three classes or castes). 8. Any rite or ceremony. 9. Funeral obsequies.

From p. 1479, *A Kannada-English Dictionary* by the Reverend F. Kittel, Mangalore, 1894

SAMSKARA

A Rite for a Dead Man

A translation of
U. R. ANANTHA MURTHY'S
Kannada novel
by
A. K. RAMANUJAN

OXFORD UNIVERSITY PRESS
New York   Oxford

Oxford University Press

Oxford   New York   Toronto
Delhi   Bombay   Calcutta   Madras   Karachi
Petaling Jaya   Singapore   Hong Kong   Tokyo
Nairobi   Dar es Salaam   Cape Town
Melbourne   Auckland

and associated companies in
Berlin   Ibadan

6 8 10 9 7

Printed in the United States of America

CONTENTS

TRANSLATOR'S NOTE

U. R. Anantha Murthy's *Samskara* is an important novel of the sixties. It is a religious novella about a decaying brahmin colony in a Karnataka village, an allegory rich in realistic detail. Popular with critic and common reader alike since its publication in 1965, it was made into an award-winning, controversial film in 1970.

Samskara takes its title seriously. Hence, our epigraph is a dictionary entry on this important Sanskrit word with many meanings. (See the Afterword for a fuller discussion.)

I have tried to make the translation self-contained, faithful yet readable. But 'the best in this kind are but shadows; and the worst are no worse, if imagination amend them'.

A translator hopes not only to translate a text, but hopes (against all odds) to translate a non-native reader into a native one. The Notes and Afterword are part of that effort.

Many friends have willingly shared their expertise and good taste with me; I wish to thank the following especially:

Girish Karnad, who checked an early draft meticulously against the original and offered detailed suggestions; U. R. Anantha Murthy, the novelist, for permission and generous criticism; Philip Oldenburg, Donald Nelson, Edward Dimock and Molly Ramanujan at Chicago, Paul Engle, Peter Nazareth and others at Iowa for commenting on drafts and sections; Shirley Payne, who typed draft after draft, with tireless goodwill; *The Illustrated Weekly of India*, for serializing the novel in their columns; the editorial staff of the Oxford University Press for reading all the proofs and for their friendship and patience.

Chicago
1976
         A. K. Ramanujan

Part One

I

He bathed Bhagirathi's body, a dried-up wasted pea-pod, and wrapped a fresh sari around it; then he offered food and flowers to the gods as he did every day, put the flowers in her hair, and gave her holy water. She touched his feet, he blessed her. Then he brought her a bowlful of cracked-wheat porridge from the kitchen.

Bhagirathi said in a low voice, 'You finish your meal first.'

'No, no. Finish your porridge. That first.'

The words were part of a twenty-year old routine between them. A routine that began with the bath at dawn, twilight prayers, cooking, medicines for his wife. And crossing the stream again to the Maruti temple for worship. That was the unfailing daily routine. After their meals, the brahmins of the agrahara would come to the front of his house, one by one, and gather there to listen to his recitation of sacred legends, always new and always dear to them and to him. In the evening he would take another bath, say more twilight prayers, make porridge for his wife, cook, eat dinner. Then there would be more recitations for the brahmins who gathered again on the verandah.

Now and then Bhagirathi would say: 'Being married to me is no joy. A house needs a child. Why don't you just get married again?' Praneshacharya would laugh aloud. 'A wedding for an old man . . .'

'Come now, what kind of an old man are you? You haven't touched forty yet. Any father would love to give you his girl and bless her with wedding water. You studied Sanskrit in Kashi. . . . A house needs a child to make it home. You've had no joy in this marriage.'

Praneshacharya would not answer. He would smile and

1

pat his wife who was trying to get up, and ask her to try and go to sleep. Didn't Lord Krishna say: Do what's to be done with no thought of fruit? The Lord definitely means to test him on his way to salvation; that's why He has given him a brahmin birth this time and set him up in this kind of family. The Acharya is filled with pleasure and a sense of worth as sweet as the five-fold nectar of holy days; he is filled with compassion for his ailing wife. He proudly swells a little at his lot, thinking, 'By marrying an invalid, I get ripe and ready.'

Before he sat down to his meal, he picked up the fodder for Gowri, the cow, on a banana leaf and placed it in front of Gowri who was grazing in the backyard. Worshipfully he caressed the cow's body, till the hair on her hide rose in pleasure. In a gesture of respect, he touched his own eyes with the hand that had touched the holy animal. As he came in, he heard a woman's voice calling out, 'Acharya, Acharya.'

It sounded like Chandri's voice. Chandri was Naranappa's concubine. If the Acharya talked to her, he would be polluted; he would have to bathe again before his meal. But how can a morsel go down the gullet with a woman waiting in the yard?

He came out. Chandri quickly pulled the end of her sari over her head, blanched, and stood there, afraid.

'What's the matter?'

'He . . . He . . .'

Chandri shivered; words stuck in her mouth. She held on to the pillar.

'What? Naranappa? What happened?'

'Gone . . .'

She covered her face with her hands.

'Narayana, Narayana—when was that?'

'Just now.'

Between sobs Chandri answered:

2

'He came back from Shivamogge and took to bed in a fever. Four days of fever, that's all. He had a painful lump on his side, the kind they get with fever.'

'Narayana.'

Praneshacharya ran out, still wrapped in the ritual raw silk, ran to Garudacharya's house and went straight to the kitchen calling out, 'Garuda, Garuda!'

The dead Naranappa had been related to Garuda for five generations. Naranappa's great-grandfather's grandmother and Garuda's great-grandfather's grandmother were sisters.

Garudacharya was in the act of raising a handful of rice mixed with *saru* to his mouth, when Praneshacharya entered, wiping the sweat of midday from his face, and said, 'Narayana. Don't. Garuda, don't eat. I hear Naranappa is dead.' Dumbstruck, Garuda threw down the mixed rice in his hand on the leaf before him, took a gulp of consecrated water and rose from his seat. He couldn't eat, even though he had quarrelled with Naranappa, severed all relations with him, and shed his kinship long ago. His wife, Sitadevi, stood there motionless, ladle in hand. He said to her, 'It's all right for the children. They can eat. Only we adults shouldn't, till the funeral rites are done.' He came out with Praneshacharya. They feared that the kinsmen next door might eat before they got the news, so they ran from house to house—Praneshacharya to Udupi Lakshmanacharya, Garudacharya to Lakshmidevamma the half-wit and to Durgabhatta down the street. The news of death spread like a fire to the other ten houses of the agrahara. Doors and windows were shut, with children inside. By god's grace, no brahmin had yet eaten. Not a human soul there felt a pang at Naranappa's death, not even women and children. Still in everyone's heart an obscure fear, an unclean anxiety. Alive, Naranappa was an enemy; dead, a preventer of meals; as a corpse, a problem, a nuisance. Soon the men moved towards the Acharya's

3

house-front. The wives blew words of warning into their husbands' ears:

'Don't be in a hurry. Wait till Praneshacharya gives you a decision. Don't agree too quickly to perform the rites. You may do the wrong thing. The guru will excommunicate you.'

The brahmins gathered again, just as they did for the daily reading of the holy legends, crowded one against the other. But today an obscure anxiety brooded among them. Fingering the basil-bead rosary round his neck, Praneshacharya said to them, almost as if to himself:

'Naranappa's death rites have to be done: that's problem one. He has no children. Someone should do it: that's problem two.'

Chandri, standing against the pillar in the yard, waited anxiously for the brahmins' verdict. The brahmin wives had come in through the backdoor into the middle hall, unable to contain their curiosity, afraid their husbands might do something rash.

Fondling his fat black naked arms, Garudacharya said as usual:

'Yes. Ye . . . es. Ye . . . es.'

'No one can eat anything until the body's cremated,' said Dasacharya, one of the poorer brahmins, thin, bony as a sick cow.

'True . . . true . . . quite true,' said Lakshmanacharya, rubbing his belly—jerking his face forwards and backwards, batting his eyelids rapidly. The only well-fed part of his body was his belly, swollen with malarial bubo. Sunken cheeks, yellow eyes deep in sockets, ribs protruding, a leg twisted—altogether an unbalanced body. The rival brahmins of Parijatapura mocked at him for walking with his buttocks out.

No one had a direct suggestion. Praneshacharya said:

'So the problem before us is—who should perform the

4

rites? The Books say, any relative can. Failing that, any brahmin can offer to do them.'

When relatives were mentioned, everyone looked at Garuda and Lakshmana. Lakshmana closed his eyes, as if to say it's not for him. But Garuda was familiar with law courts, having walked up and down many; he felt it was his turn to speak up. So he raised a pinch of snuff to his nose and cleared his throat:

'It's but right we should go by the ancient Law Books. Acharya, you are our greatest scholar, your word is vedic gospel to us. Give us the word, we'll do it. Between Naranappa and me, it's true, there's a bond of kinship going back several generations. But, as you know, his father and I fought over that orchard and went to court. After his father's death, I appealed to the guru at the Dharmasthala monastery. He decreed in my favour. Yet Naranappa defied it, even god's word—what do you say?—So we swore we'd have nothing between us for generations to come, nothing, no exchange of words, no wedding, no rite, no meal, no hospitality. That's what we swore—what do you say . . .'

Gurudacharya's nasal sentences punctuated by his what-do-you-says suddenly halted, but were spurred on again by two more pinches of snuff. He gathered courage, looked around, saw Chandri's face and said boldly:

'The guru will also agree to what you say. What do you say? Let's set aside the question of whether I should do the rites. The real question is: is he a brahmin at all? What do you say?—He slept regularly with a lowcaste woman . . .'

There was only one man from the Smarta sect, Durgabhatta, in this colony of Madhva brahmins. He was always checking and measuring the rival sect's orthodoxy with a questioning eye. He looked sideways at Chandri and cackled:

'Chi Chi Chi, don't be too rash, Acharya. O no, a brahmin isn't lost because he takes a lowborn prostitute. Our ances-

5

tors after all came from the North—you can ask Praneshacharya if you wish—history says they cohabited with Dravidian women. Don't think I am being facetious. Think of all the people who go to the brothels of Basrur in South Kanara . . .'

Garudacharya got angry. This fellow was mischievous.

'Not so fast, not so fast, Durgabhatta! The question here is not simply one of carnal desire. We don't have to advise our great Praneshacharya. He knows all about alliances and misalliances, has studied it all in Kashi, he knows all the scriptures, earned the title Crest-Jewel of Vedic Learning. What do you say? . . . Our Acharya has won all sorts of arguments with all the super-pundits, yours and ours, won honours at every seat of learning in the South, fifteen lace shawls and silver platters . . . our Acharya . . . what do you say? . . .'

Embarrassed by the way this conversation had turned away from the question at hand towards his own praise, Praneshacharya said:

'Lakshmana, what do *you* say? Naranappa was married to your wife's sister, after all.'

Lakshmana closed his eyes.

'It's your word, your command. What do we know of the subtleties of dharma? As Garuda says, Naranappa had contacts with a lowcaste . . .' He stopped in the middle of his sentence, opened his eyes wide, and dug into his nose with his upper cloth. 'As you know, he even ate what she cooked . . .'

Padmanabhacharya who lived right opposite Naranappa's house added:

'And he drank too.'

'Besides drinking, he ate animal flesh.' Turning to Durgabhatta, Garudacharya said, 'Maybe even that doesn't matter too much to *you* people. Shankara, your great founder, in his hunger for full experience, exchanged his body for a dead

6

king's and enjoyed himself with the queen, didn't he?'

Praneshacharya thought that the talk was getting out of hand. He said, 'Garuda. Stop talking for a while, please.'

'Naranappa abandoned his lawful wife after tying the wedding-string round her neck. You may condone even that . . .' Lakshmana had closed his eyes again and started talking. 'He went and got mixed up with some woman. My wife's sister became hysterical and died: he didn't even come to the funeral rites. You may condone even that; but he didn't care to observe the death anniversaries of his own father and mother. I'm not the sort who would hide anything about him just because he was my close relative. He was my wife's uncle's son. We tolerated things and sheltered him in our lap as long as we could. In return, what does he do? He comes to the river in full view of all the brahmins and takes the holy stone that we've worshipped for generations and throws it in the water and spits after it! Condone everything if you wish —but didn't he, wilfully, before our very eyes, bring Muslims over and eat and drink forbidden things in the wide-open front yard? If any of us questioned him in good faith, he would turn on us, cover us with abuse from head to foot. As long as he lived, we just had to walk in fear of him.'

Lakshmana's wife, Anasuya, listening to him from inside the house, felt proud that her husband said all the right things. Her eyes fell on Chandri sitting against the pillar, and she cursed her to her heart's content: may tigers trample her at midnight, may snakes bite her, this whore, this seducing witch! If she had not given him potions, why should he, Anasuya's own maternal uncle's son, why should he push aside his own kinswoman, call her an invalid, squander all his property, and throw all the ancestral gold and jewels on the neck of this evil witch! She looked at the four-strand gold chain round Chandri's neck and the thick gold bracelet on her wrist, and could not bear to think of it. She wept

7

loudly. If only her sister had been alive, that gold chain would have been round *her* neck—would a blood-relative's corpse lie around like this without even the benefit of a rite? All because of this filthy whore—won't someone brand her face! Anasuya simmered and simmered till she boiled over and cried.

Dasacharya lived entirely on the meals that brahmins get at death-rites and anniversaries. He would walk ten miles for such a meal any day. He complained: 'As you all know, we let him stay in our agarahara, so for two whole years we didn't get calls for any meal or banquet. If we do the rites for him now or anything rash like that, no one will ever invite us for a brahmin meal. But then we can't keep his dead body uncremated here in the agrahara either, and fast for ever. This is a terrible dilemma. Praneshacharya should tell us precisely what's right and what's wrong. Who in our sect can dispute his word?'

For Durgabhatta, this was an internal issue. He sat unconcerned in his place, ogling Chandri. For the first time his connoisseur eyes had the chance to appraise this precious object which did not normally stir out of the house, this choice object that Naranappa had brought from Kundapura. A real 'sharp' type, exactly as described in Vatsyayana's manual of love—look at her, toes longer than the big toe, just as the Love Manual says. Look at those breasts. In sex she's the type who sucks the male dry. Her eyes, which should be fickle, are now misty with grief and fear, but she looks good that way. Like Matsyagandhi, the Fisherwoman in the Ravi Varma print hung up in Durgabhatta's bedroom, shyly trying to hide her breasts bursting through her poor rag of a sari. The same eyes and nose: no wonder Naranappa threw away the worship-stone for her, ate taboo meat and drank taboo liquor. One wonders at his daring. One remembers Jagannatha the brahmin poet who married the Muslim girl,

8

and his verses about the alien's breasts. If Praneshacharya were not present, if Naranappa weren't lying dead right there, he would have happily quoted the stanza and expanded on it even to these barren brahmins. 'To the lustful'—that is, to Naranappa and his like—'there's no fear, no shame', as the saying goes.

Noticing that the audience was silent, Durgabhatta spoke up:

'We've anyway said whatever needs to be said. What's the use of raking up dead men's faults? Let Praneshacharya speak. He is a guru, for me as for you, regardless of what Garudacharya may say in his passion.'

Praneshacharya was weighing every word, knowing full well that the protection of the entire brahmin agrahara was now on his shoulders. He spoke haltingly.

'Garuda said: an oath stands between him and Naranappa. Yet the Books of Law have ways of absolving such oaths— you can perform a rite of absolution, give away a cow, make a pilgrimage. But this is an expensive matter, and I've no right to ask anyone to spend his money. And as for the question raised by Lakshmana and Dasa and others that Naranappa didn't behave as a well-born brahmin, that he's a smear on the good name of the agrahara, it's a deep question—I have no clear answer. For one thing, he may have rejected brahminhood, but brahminhood never left him. No one ever excommunicated him officially. He didn't die an outcaste; so he remains a brahmin in his death. Only another brahmin has any right to touch his body. If we let someone else do it, we'd be sullying our brahminhood. Yet I hesitate, I can't tell you dogmatically: go ahead with the rite. I hesitate because you've all seen the way he lived. What shall we do? What do the Law Books really say, is there any real absolution for such violations? . . .'

Suddenly Chandri did something that stunned the brahmins. She moved forward to stand in the front courtyard. They couldn't believe their own eyes: Chandri loosened her four-strand gold chain, her thick bracelet, her bangles, and placed them all in a heap before Praneshacharya. She mumbled something about all this jewelry being there for the expenses of the rite, and went back to stand in her place.

The women calculated swiftly: that heap of gold was worth at least two thousand rupees. One after another, the wives scanned their husbands' faces. The brahmins bowed their heads: they were afraid, fearful that the lust for gold might destroy brahmin purity. But in the heart of every one of them flashed the question: if some other brahmin should perform the final rite for Naranappa, he might keep his brahminhood and yet put all that gold on his wife's neck. The new reason inflamed further the jealous hatred between Lakshmana and Garuda: 'Suppose this wretch should rake in all that gold giving a poor starving cow as a token gift, insuring both the goods of this world and the other?' Durgabhatta said to himself: 'If these Madhvas get tempted and cremate Naranappa, I'll roam the towns, spread the news, expose these so-called brahmins.' The eyes of the poorer brahmins like Dasa grew moist, their mouths watered. Would Garuda and Lakshmana let anyone else do the rites?

Praneshacharya grew anxious. Why did Chandri spoil everything with her good intentions?

Every brahmin present was afraid that someone else might be tempted to agree, and vied with the others in lurid accounts of Naranappa's misdeeds—things done not to them but always to others.

'Who induced Garuda's son to run away from home and join the army? Naranappa, who else? Praneshacharya had taught the boy the Vedic scriptures, but what mattered finally was only Naranappa's word. That fellow was hell-bent on corrupting our young people . . .'

10

'Look at poor Lakshmana's son-in-law now. Lakshmana picks an orphan, nurses him, brings him up and gives his daughter in marriage to him—then Naranappa comes along and turns the young fellow's head. You hardly see him here once in a month.'

'And then those fish in the temple-pond. For generations they were dedicated to Lord Ganesha. People believe that anyone who catches the sacred fish will vomit blood and die. But this outcaste scoundrel didn't care two hoots, he got together his Muslim gang, dynamited the tank and killed off god's own fish. Now even lowcaste folk go there and fish. The rascal undermined all good brahmin influence on the others, he saw to it. And then, he wasn't content with ruining our agrahara, he had to go and spoil the boys of Parijatapura too, make them run after dramas and shows.'

'The casteless scoundrel should have been excommunicated, what do you say?'

'How could that be Garuda? He threatened to become a Muslim. On the eleventh day of the moon, when every brahmin was fasting, he brought in Muslims to the agrahara and feasted them. He said, "Try and excommunicate me now. I'll become a Muslim, I'll get you all tied to pillars and cram cow's flesh into your mouths and see to it personally that your sacred brahminism is ground into the mud." He said that. If he had really become a Muslim no law could have thrown him out of the brahmin agrahara. We would have had to leave. Even Praneshacharya kept quiet then, his hands were tied too.'

Dasacharya put in his last word. He was upset he'd had to get up from his meal before he'd a chance to taste one morsel of his mango-rice. He was hungry.

'After his father's death, no brahmin here got a taste of that jackfruit in his backyard—and it used to taste like honey.'

11

The women kept staring at the heap of gold and they were disappointed by their husbands' words. Garuda's wife, Sita, was outraged by the way Lakshmana had shot his mouth off about her son joining the army. What right did *he* have to talk about her son? Lakshmana's wife, Anasuya, was outraged by Garuda talking about *her* son-in-law being corrupted —what right did he have?

Thinking what an ordeal this whole affair was getting to be, Praneshacharya said almost in soliloquy:

'What's the way out now? Can we just fold our arms and stare at a dead body laid out in the agrahara? According to ancient custom, until the body is properly removed there can be no worship, no bathing, no prayers, no food, nothing. And, because he was not excommunicated, no one but a brahmin can touch his body.'

'Not excommunicating him at the right time—that's the cause of all this mess,' said Garuda, who for years had screamed for an excommunication. He got his chance now to say, 'I-told-you-so, you-didn't-listen-to-me.'

The brahmins countered him as one man: 'Yes, yes, if he had actually become a Muslim, we'd have had to leave the polluted agrahara; there'd have been no two ways about it.'

Dasa, who had meanwhile been imagining the hardship of a whole day without food, suddenly came out with an idea. He stood up alertly and said:

'I have heard that Naranappa was very friendly with the brahmins of Parijatapura. They ate and hobnobbed together. Why don't we ask them? Their orthodoxy is not as strict as ours, anyway.'

Parijatapura's brahmins were Smartas, not quite out of the upper set, their lines being a little mixed. Once upon a time some lecher got one of their widows pregnant and their agrahara tried to hush it up. The rumour was that the guru at Shringeri heard of it and excommunicated the whole colony.

12

On the whole the brahmins of Parijatapura were pleasure-lovers, not so crazy about orthodoxy and strict rules; they were experts at running betelnut farms, and rich too. So, Durgabhatta had a soft spot for the whole clan; further-more, he was a Smarta himself. He had secretly eaten their flat-rice and *uppittu* and drunk their coffee. He was not brazen enough to eat a whole meal with them, that's all.

Furthermore, he was fascinated by their widows who didn't shave their heads and grew their hair long, who even chewed betel leaf and reddened their mouths. He got into quite a rage at Dasacharya—'Look at this Madhva's gall, though he can't afford a morning meal.' He stood up and said:

'Look, that's a foul thing to say. You may think them low hybrid brahmins, but they don't think so themselves. If your sect will be polluted by laying hands on your own dead man, wouldn't it pollute them worse? Go ahead, be cheeky and ask them—you'll get an earful. Do you know that Manjayya of Parijatapura has enough money to buy up every man's son here?'

Praneshacharya tried to pacify Durgabhatta's anger.

'You're quite right. It's not truly brahminical to get some-one else to do what you don't do yourself. But friendship is as strong a bond as blood, isn't it? If they and Naranappa were friends, don't you think they should be told of their good friend's death?'

Durgabhatta said, 'Agreed, Acharya. The brahminism of your entire sect is in your hands. Your burden is great. Who can go against what you decide?' He had spoken all he felt. He didn't speak again.

The question of the gold ornaments came up again. If the Parijatapura people chose to perform the rites, shouldn't the gold go to them? Lakshmana's wife, Anasuya, could not bear the thought of her sister's rightful jewels falling into the

13

hands of some hybrid brahmin in the next village. Unable to contain herself any more, she blurted out: 'Who does she think she is? If things were straight, they should be around my sister's neck.' Then she broke into sobs. Lakshmana felt the rightness of his wife's words, but he didn't want his status as a husband to be lowered in public. So he snarled, 'You shut up now. Why are you prating in an assembly of menfolk?'

Garuda, angry now, thundered: 'What kind of talk is this? According to the decree of the Dharmasthala guru, this gold belongs to me.'

Wearily Praneshacharya consoled them.

'Be patient. What's before us is a dead body waiting to be cremated. About the gold—leave the decision to me. First send someone to Parijatapura with the news. If they decide by themselves to perform the rites, let them.'

Then he stood up and said, 'You may go now. I'll look into Manu and other texts. I'll see if there's a way out of this dilemma.' Chandri pulled her sari-end over her head respectfully, and looked imploringly at the Acharya.

II

There were cockroaches in the buttermilk shelves, fat rats in the store-room. In the middle room, ritually washed saris and clothes hung out on a rope stretched for a clothes-line. Fresh *pappadams*, fries, and marinated red peppers spread out to dry on the verandah mat. Sacred balsam plants in the backyard. These were common to all the houses in the agrahara. The differences were only in the flowering trees in the backyards: Bhimacharya had *parijata*, Padmanabhacharya had a jasmine bush, Lakshmana had the ember-*champak*, Garuda had red *ranja*, Dasa had white *mandara*. Durgabhatta had the conch-flower and the *bilva* leaf for Shiva-worship. The brahmins went to each other's yards each morning to get flowers for worship and to ask after each other's welfare. But the flowers that bloomed in Naranappa's yard were reserved solely for Chandri's hair and for a vase in the bedroom. As if that wasn't provocative enough, right in his front yard grew a bush, a favourite of snakes, with flowers unfit for any god's crown—the night-queen bush. In the darkness of night, the bush was thickly clustered with flowers, invading the night like some raging lust, pouring forth its nocturnal fragrance. The agrahara writhed in its hold as in the grip of a magic serpent-binding spell. People with delicate nostrils complained of headaches, walked about with their dhotis held to their noses. Some clever fellows even said Naranappa had grown the bush to guard with snakes the gold he had gathered. While the auspicious brahmin wives, with their dwarfish braids and withered faces, wore *mandara* and jasmine, Chandri wore her black-snake hair coiled in a knot and wore the flowers of the ember-*champak* and the heady fragrant screw-pine. All day the smells were gentle and tranquil, the sandalpaste on the brahmins' bodies and the soft fragrance of *parijata* and other such flowers. But when it grew dark, the night-queen reigned over the agrahara.

The jackfruit and mango in the backyard of each house tasted different from all the others. The fruit and flower were distributed, according to the saying: 'Share fruit and eat it, share flowers and wear them'. Only Lakshmana was sneaky, he moved out half the yield of his trees and sold it to the Konkani shopkeepers. His was a niggard's spirit. Whenever his wife's people came visiting, he watched his wife's hands with the eyes of a hawk—never sure when or what she was passing on to her mother's house. In the hot months every house put out *kosumbari*-salads and sweet fruit-drinks; in the eighth month they invited each other for lamp-offerings. Naranappa was the only exception to all these exchanges. A total of ten houses stood on either side of the agrahara street. Naranappa's house, bigger than the others, stood at one end. The Tunga river flowed close to the backyards of the houses on one side of the street, with steps to get down to the water, steps built by some pious soul long ago. In the rainy month the river would rise, roar for three or four days, making as if she was going to rush into the agarahara; offer a carnival of swirls and water-noises for the eyes and ears of children, and then subside. By mid-summer she would dry to a mere rustle, a trickle of three strands of water. Then the brahmins raised green and yellow cucumber or water-melon in the sand-bank as vegetables for rainy days. All twelve months of the year colourful cucumbers hung from the ceiling, wrapped in banana-fibre. In the rainy season, they used cucumber for everything, curry, mash, or soup made with the seeds; and like pregnant women, the brahmins longed for the soups of sour mango-mash. All twelve months of the year, they had vows to keep; they had calls for ritual meals occasioned by deaths, weddings, young boys' initiations. On big festival days, like the day of the annual temple celebrations or the death-anniversary of the Great Commentator, there would be a feast in the monastery thirty miles away. The brahmins' lives ran smoothly in this annual cycle of appointments.

The name of the agrahara was Durvasapura. There was a place-legend about it. Right in the middle of the flowing Tunga river stood an island-like hillock, overgrown with a knot of trees. They believed Sage Durvasa still performed his penance on it. In the Second Aeon of the cycle of time, for a short while, the five Pandava brothers had lived ten miles from here, in a place called Kaimara. Once their wife Draupadi had wanted to go for a swim in the water. Bhima,

16

a husband who fulfilled every whim of his wife, had dammed
up the Tunga river for her. When Sage Durvasa woke up in
the morning and looked for water for his bath and prayers,
there wasn't any in his part of the Tunga. He got angry. But
Dharmaraja, the eldest, with his divine vision, could see
what was happening, and advised his rash brother Bhima to
do something about it. Bhima, son of the wind-god, forever
obedient to this elder brother's words, broke the dam in three
places and let the water flow. That's why even today from
the Kaimara dam on, the river flows in three strands. The
brahmins of Durvasapura often say to their neighbouring
agraharas: on the twelfth day of the moon, early in the morning, any truly pious man could hear the conch of Sage Durvasa from his clump of trees. But the brahmins of the
agrahara never made any crude claims that they themselves
had ever heard the sound of that conch.

So, the agrahara had become famous in all ten directions
—because of its legends, and also because of Praneshacharya,
the great ascetic, 'Crest-Jewel of Vedic Learning', who had
settled down there, and certainly because of that scoundrel
Naranappa. On special occasions like the birth-anniversary
of Lord Rama, people mobbed the place from the neighbouring agraharas to hear Praneshacharya's ancient holy
tales. Though Naranappa was a problem, the Acharya nursed
his invalid wife to uphold the great mercy of god, bore up
with Naranappa's misdeeds, dispersed little by little the darkness in the brahmins' heads filled with chants they did not
understand. His duties in this world grew lighter and more
fragrant like sandalwood rubbed daily on stone.

The agrahara street was hot, so hot you could pop corn on
it. The brahmins walked through it, weak with hunger, their
heads covered with their upper cloth; they crossed the three-
pronged river and entered the cool forest to reach Parijata-

pura after an hour's trudging. The green of the betelnut grove lifted the earth's coolness to the heat of the sky. In the airless atmosphere the trees were still. Hot dust burned the brahmins' feet. Invoking Lord Narayana's name, they entered Manjayya's house in which they had never set foot before. Manjayya, a rich man shrewd in wordly affairs, was writing accounts. He spoke loudly and offered right and proper courtesies.

'Oh oh oh, the entire brahmin clan seems to have found its way here. Please come in, please be good enough to sit down. Wouldn't you like to relax a bit, maybe wash your feet? . . . Look here, bring some plantains for the guests, will you?'

His wife brought ripe plantains on a platter, and said, 'Please come in.' They thanked her politely, and went in, Garuda made a hissing sound as he sat down and mentioned Naranappa's death.

'O God. What happened to him? He was here eight or nine days ago on some business. Said he was going to Shivamogge. Asked me if I wanted anything done. I asked him to find out if the markets had sold any arecanuts. Shiva, Shiva. . . . He had said he'd be back by Thursday. What, was he sick? With what?'

Dasacharya said, 'Just four days of fever—he also had a swelling.'

'Shiva, Shiva,' exclaimed Manjayya, as he closed his eyes and fanned himself. Knowing Shivamogge town as he did, he suddenly remembered the one-syllable name of the dread epidemic; and not daring to utter it even to himself, merely said, 'Shiva, Shiva'.

In the blink of an eye, all the lower-caste brahmins of Parijatapura gathered on the bund.

'You know—' began Garuda, shrewd man of the world, 'we agrahara people had a bad fight with Naranappa, we didn't exchange even water and rice. But you here were all

18

his friends, what do you say, now he's dead, his rites have to be done, what do you say? . . .'

The Parijatapura folks were unhappy over their friend's death, but quite happy they were getting a chance to cremate a highcaste brahmin. They were partly pleased because Naranappa ate in their houses with no show of caste pride.

Shankarayya, priest of Parijatapura, intervened. 'According to brahmin thinking, "a snake is also a twice-born"; if you happen to see a dead snake, you've to perform the proper rites for it; you shouldn't eat till you've done so. As that's the case, it's absolutely wrong to sit back with folded arms when a brahmin has passed on to the bosom of God. Don't you think so?'

He said this really to display his knowledge of the texts, to tell those Madhvas 'we here are no less than you', and to bring down their pride.

Durgabhatta was very agitated by this man's words.

'Look at this stupid brahmin, rashly opening his stupid mouth. He'll bring a bad name to the whole Smarta clan,' he thought, and spoke in his own crooked way.

'Yes yes yes, we understand all that. That's exactly what Praneshacharya also says. But our dilemma is something else: is Naranappa, who drank liquor and ate meat, who threw the holy stone into the river, is he a brahmin or is he not? Tell me, which of us is willing to lose his brahminhood here? Yet it's not at all right, I agree, to keep a dead brahmin's body waiting, uncremated.'

Shankarayya's heart panicked and missed a beat. His clan had already been classed low, and he didn't like them to fall lower by doing something unbrahminical. So he said:

'If that's so, wait, we can't do anything rash. You, of course, have in Praneshacharya a man known all over the South. Let him look into it and tell us what's right in this crisis. He can untangle the delicate strands of right and wrong.'

19

But Manjayya didn't hesitate to say, 'Don't worry about the expenses. Wasn't he my friend? I'll personally see to it that all the necessary charities etcetera are done,' meaning really to jibe at the niggardly Madhva crowd.

III

When the brahmins left for Parijatapura, Praneshacharya asked Chandri to sit down, came into the dining-room where his wife lay, and proceeded to tell her how pure Chandri's heart was, how she'd laid down all her gold and what new complications arose from that generous act. Then he sat down among his palm-leaf texts, riffling them for the right and lawful answer. As far back as he could remember Naranappa had always been a problem. The real challenge was to test which would finally win the agrahara: his own penance and faith in ancient ways, or Naranappa's demoniac ways. He wondered by what evil influence Naranappa had got this way, and prayed that god's grace should bring him redemption. The Acharya fasted two nights in the week for him. His painful concern and compassion for Naranappa had stemmed also from a promise he had made to the dead man's mother. He had consoled the dying woman: 'I'll take care of your son's welfare, and bring him to the right paths. Don't worry about him.' But Naranappa hadn't walked the path, he had turned a deaf ear to all counsel. By sheer power of example, he'd even stolen Praneshacharya's own wards and Sanskrit pupils—Garuda's son Shyama, Lakshmana's son-in-law Shripati. Naranappa had incited Shyama to run away from home and join the army. The Acharya, wearied by complaints, had gone to see Naranappa one day. He was lolling on a soft mattress, and showed some courtesy by getting up. He didn't take counsel well, and talked his head off;

20

sneered at the Acharya and brahmin ways.

'Your texts and rites don't work any more The Congress Party is coming to power, you'll have to open up the temples to all outcastes,' and so on irreverently.

The Acharya had even said, 'Stop it, it isn't good for you. Don't separate Shripati from his wife.'

A guffaw was the answer. 'O Acharya, who in the world can live with a girl who gives no pleasure—except of course some barren brahmins!' 'You fellows—you brahmins—you want to tie me down to a hysterical female, just because she is some relative, right? Just keep your dharma to yourself—we've but one life—I belong to the "Hedonist School" which says—borrow, if you must, but drink your ghee.'

The Acharya pleaded, 'Do whatever you want to do yourself. Please, please don't corrupt these boys.'

He just laughed. 'Your Garuda, he robs shaven widows, he plots evil with black magic men, and he is one of your brahmins, isn't he? . . . All right, let's see who wins, Acharya. You or me? Let's see how long all this brahmin business will last. All your brahmin respectability. I'll roll it up and throw it all ways for a little bit of pleasure with one female. You better leave now—I don't really want to talk and hurt you either', he said finally.

Why had he, the Acharya, objected to excommunicating such a creature? Was it fear, or compassion? Or the obstinate thought he could win some day? Anyway, here is Naranappa testing out his brahminhood in death, as he did in life.

The last time he saw Naranappa was three months ago, one evening on the fourteenth day of the moon. Garuda had brought in a complaint. Naranappa had taken Muslims with him that morning to the Ganapati temple stream, and before everyone's eyes he'd caught and carried away the sacred fish. Those free-swimming man-length fish, they came to the banks and ate rice from the hand—if any man caught them

21

he would cough up blood and die. At least that's what everyone believed. Naranappa had broken the taboo. The Acharya
was afraid of the bad example. With this kind of rebellious
example, how will fair play and righteousness prevail? Won't
the lower castes get out of hand? In this decadent age, common men follow the right paths out of fear—if that were
destroyed, where could we find the strength to uphold the
world? He had to speak out. So he had walked quickly to
Naranappa's place and confronted him on the verandah.

Naranappa was probably drunk; his eyes were bloodshot,
his hair was dishevelled. And yet, didn't he, as soon as he
saw the Acharya, put a cloth to his mouth?

The Acharya felt a dawning of hope when he saw this
gesture of respect and fear. He sometimes felt that Naranappa's nature was a tricky maze he had no way of entering.
But here in this gesture, he saw a crack, a chink in the man's
demoniac pride, and felt his forces of virtue rush towards
him.

He knew that words were useless. He knew, unless his
goodness flowed like the Ganges silently into Naranappa, he
would not become open. Yet, a desire welled up in the
Acharya, a lust, to swoop on Naranappa like a sacred eagle,
to shake him up, tear open the inward springs of ambrosia
till they really flowed.

He looked at Naranappa cruelly. Any ordinary sinner
would have been terror-struck and fallen to the ground under
that gaze. Just two repentant drops from this sinner's eyes,
and that would be enough: he'd hug him as a brother—and
he looked at Naranappa with desire.

Naranappa bowed his head. He looked as if the sacred
bird of prey had swooped and held him in its talons, as if
he'd been turned to a worm that minute, bewildered as when
a closed door suddenly opens.

Yet, no; he put aside the cloth that covered his mouth,

threw it on the chair, and laughed out aloud:

'Chandri! Where's the bottle? Let's give the Acharya a little of this holy water!'

'Shut up!' Praneshacharya was shaking from head to foot. He was angered at the way the man slipped from under his influence, and felt he had missed a step on the stairs he was descending.

'Aha! The Acharya too can get angry! Lust and anger, I thought, were only for the likes of us. But then anger plays on the nose-tips of people who try to hold down lust. That's what they say. Durvasa, Parashara, Bhrigu, Brihaspati, Kashyapa, all the sages were given to anger. Chandri, where's the bottle? Look, Acharya—those are the great sages who set the tradition, right? Quite a lusty lot, those sages. What was the name of the fellow who ravished the fisherwoman smelling of fish, right in the boat and gave her body a permanent perfume? And now, look at these poor brahmins, descended from such sages!'

'Naranappa, shut your mouth.'

Naranappa, now angry that Chandri didn't bring the liquor to him, ran upstairs making a big noise, brought the bottle down and filled his cup. Chandri tried to stop him, but he pushed her aside. Praneshacharya closed his eyes and tried to leave.

'Acharya, stop, stay a while,' said Naranappa. Praneshacharya stayed, mechanically; if he left now he would seem to be afraid. The stench of liquor disgusted him. 'Listen,' said Naranappa in a voice of authority. Taking a draught from his cup, he laughed wickedly.

'Let's see who wins in the end—you or me. I'll destroy brahminism, I certainly will. My only sorrow is that there's no brahminism really left to destroy in this place—except you. Garuda, Lakshmana, Durgabhatta—ahaha—what brahmins! If I were still a brahmin, that fellow Garudacharya

23

would have washed me down with his *aposhana* water. Or that Lakshmana—he loves money so much he'll lick a copper coin off a heap of shit. He will tie another wilted sister-in-law round my neck, just to get at my property. And I'd have had to cut my hair to a tuft, smear charcoal on my face, sit on your verandah and listen to your holy-holy yarns.'

Naranappa took another draught and belched. Chandri stood inside watching everything fearfully, folded her hands and gestured to the Acharya to go away. Praneshacharya turned to go—what's the point of talking with a drunkard?

'Acharya, listen to this. Why this vanity, why should the agrahara listen to your words all the time? Why don't you listen to a thing or two I say? I'll tell you a holy yarn myself.

'Once, in an agrahara, there lived a very holy Achari—that is, once upon a time. His wife was always ill and he didn't know what it was to have pleasure with a woman—but his lustre, his fame had travelled far and wide to many towns. The other brahmins in the agrahara were awful sinners—they knew every kind of sin, sins of gluttony, sins of avarice, love of gold. But then, this Achari's terrific virtue covered up all their sins; so they sinned some more. As the Achari's virtue grew, so did the sins of everyone else in the agrahara. One day a funny thing happened. What, Acharya-re, are you listening? There's a moral at the end—every action results not in what is expected but in its exact opposite. Listen to the lesson and you can go tell the other brahmins too.

'Here comes the funny part. There was a young fellow in the agrahara. He never once slept with his one lawfully wedded wife because she wouldn't sleep with him—out of sheer obedience to her mother's orders. But this young man didn't miss an evening of this Achari's recitations of holy legends—every evening he was there. He'd good reason. It's true, that Achari had no direct experience of life, but he was quite a sport with erotic poetry and things like that. One day

24

he got into a description of Kalidasa's heroine, Shakuntala, in some detail. This young man listened. He was already disgusted with his wife, because the stupid girl complained to her mother that he came to her bed only to pinch her at night. But now the young man felt the Achari's description in his own body, felt a whole female grow inside him, a fire burn in his loins—you know what it means, don't you, Acharya-re?—He couldn't stand it, he leapt from the Achari's verandah and ran. He couldn't bear to hear any more, he ran straight to plunge his heat in the cold water of the river. Luckily, an outcaste woman was bathing there, in the moonlight. Luckily, too, she wasn't wearing too much, all the limbs and parts he craved to see were right before his eyes. She certainly was the fish-scented fisherwoman type, the type your great sage fell for. He fantasied she was the Shakuntala of the Achari's description and this pure brahmin youth made love to her right there—with the moon for witness.

'Now, you explicate it, Acharya-re—didn't the Achari himself corrupt the brahminism of the place? Did he or didn't he? That's why our elders always said: read the Vedas, read the Puranas, but don't try to interpret them. Acharya-re, you are the one who's studied in Kashi—you tell me, who ruined brahminism?'

As Praneshacharya stood silently listening to Naranappa's words, he began to worry: is this a drunkard's rigmarole? Could it be he himself was responsible for such awful things?

With a sigh, he said: 'Only sin has a tongue, virtue has none. God have mercy on you—that's all.'

'You read those lush sexy Puranas, but you preach a life of barrenness. But my words, they say what they mean: if I say *sleep with a woman*, it means *sleep with a woman*; if I say *eat fish*, it means *eat fish*. Can I give you brahmins a piece of

25

advice, Acharya-re? Push those sickly wives of yours into the river. Be like the sages of your holy legends—get hold of a fish-scented fisherwoman who can cook you fish-soup, and go to sleep in her arms. And if you don't experience god when you wake up, my name isn't Naranappa.' Then he winked at the Acharya, quaffed the liquor in his cup and let out a loud long belch.

The Acharya, angered by Naranappa's sneering at his invalid wife, scolded him, called him a low-born scoundrel, and came home. That night, when he sat down for his prayers, he couldn't 'still the waves of his mind'. He said, 'O God', in distress. He gave up telling the luscious Puranic stories in the evenings and started on moral tales of penance. The result—his own enthusiasm for reciting the Puranas faded and died. The young listeners who used to look at him with lively eyes and bring joy to his heart, stopped coming. Only women bent on earning merit, uttering the names of god over yawns in the middle of the stories, and old old men, were his audience now.

As he sat reading and contemplating his palm-leaves, he heard his wife's moan and remembered he hadn't given her the afternoon's medicine. He brought it in a small cup, and leaning her head against his chest, poured it into her mouth, and said, 'You'd better sleep now.' He came back into the hall, muttering to himself obstinately, 'What do I mean by saying there's no answer to this dilemma in the Books?' And started reading through them again.

IV

The brahmins came back from Parijatapura, muttering 'Hari Hari Hari' as they walked hungry in the sun, thinking of a little rest in the afternoon. But the wives, especially Garuda's wife and Lakshmana's, wouldn't let them rest, and treated them to the Lord's Counsel.

In the agrahara they gave all sorts of reasons why Garuda's single son and heir, Shyama, had run away from home and joined the army. Garuda's enemies said, that the son couldn't take his father's punishments any more. Naranappa's enemies said he had incited Shyama to join the army. Lakshmana's opinion was different—the black magic Garuda used against Naranappa's father must have boomeranged back on himself, why else should Shyama go wrong and run away in spite of Praneshacharya's teaching? Anyone who uses black magic, like the Ash-Demon who wanted to burn his own creator, ends up burning himself. Lakshmana's wife, Anasuya, smarting over Naranappa who had sullied her mother's family name, used to blame him also on Garuda: if Garuda didn't resort to black magic why would a well-born man like Naranappa have gone astray and become an outcaste?

Garuda's wife, Sitadevi, had given up food and drink, and pined away, for her son was 'ruined by that scoundrel Naranappa'. She'd waited night and day, and groaned for three months. At last a letter came from Shyama—he was in Poona, had joined the army. He was bonded to them by a signature on legal paper, so he couldn't leave unless he put down six hundred rupees as penalty. After that Sitadevi had accosted Naranappa on the street, her arms akimbo, and scolded and wept. Then she'd got a letter written to her son saying, 'Don't ever eat meat, don't give up your baths and twilight prayers.' She'd fasted Friday nights so that her son's heart might turn good and clean. Garudacharya had raged like Durvasa, and jumped about as if overrun by red ants, shouting, 'He's as good as dead to me, if he so much as shows his face here I'll break his head.' Sitadevi had offered vows to the goddess: 'Give my husband peace, may his love be constant for his son.' And had given up her food even on Satur-

27

day nights. Durgabhatta, that hater of Madhvas, had fuelled the already burning fire, shaming Garuda into lying low forever, by saying, 'He's in the army, he'll have no baths, no prayers; and they'll force him to eat meat now.'

Today Sitadevi came home happy thinking they might even be able to buy off her son from the military bond, if only Chandri's jewelry came into their hands. The Law Books must have it somewhere that her husband could perform Naranappa's rites. But she was worried. Would Lakshmana forestall her own husband and offer to do the rites?—Or those people of Parijatapura? They seemed to have no sense of pollution at all, clean and unclean seemed all one to them. She vowed offerings of fruit and coconut to Maruti—'O God, please let my husband be the one to do the rites, please.' Now, Naranappa's meat-eating didn't look too heinous. One of these days her son would return from the army—will the cruel tongues of the agrahara keep quiet about it? What'll happen if he gets excommunicated? She'd once maligned Praneshacharya for hesitating to excommunicate Naranappa. Now she thought of him worshipfully: he's truly a man of lovingkindness, surely he'll take on her son's sins also and protect him. No doubt about it.

Garudacharya had hardly come home and tried to rest on the floor when Sitadevi began to nag him tearfully. But he said severely, 'To me he's as good as dead. Don't let me hear a word about that scoundrel.' Yet his wife's suggestion entered him like a tick and troubled him. Let everything go to hell, let his son go to hell, he wasn't ready to kill his brahminhood. Yet if only Praneshacharya would say 'Yes', the path would be clear. Then he could even rescue his only son and heir from the army. Only a son could offer his fatherly soul any consolations after death.

Though he had growled at his wife 'Shut up, impossible,' Garuda stepped like a thief into Praneshacharya's house.

Without looking at the face of Chandri who was sitting on the raised verandah, he walked into the middle hall.

'Sit down, Garuda. I hear that the Parijatapura folks said they'd do as the Books say. That's right, of course,' said Praneshacharya and returned to his palm-leaves. Garuda cleared his throat and asked:

'What do Manu's *Laws* say, Acharya-re?'

Praneshacharya silently shook his head. Garuda went on.

'Sir, what's there in the Books that *you* don't know? I am not asking you about that. Haven't I heard you in contro-versy with great pundits—what do you say—in the monastery that day—what do you say—on the death-anniversary of the Great Commentator—argue with those pundits from the Vyasaraya monastery? Those fellows were beaten by your challenge—to interpret the sentence, "Thou art the Original, and me the reflection"—according to our Madhva school. The feast that day went on for four hours. So you mustn't misunderstand me; I haven't come to offer *you* any sugges-tions. In your presence, I'm a lout, a clumsy bear.'

The Acharya felt disgust rising in him at Garuda's attempts to flatter and cajole him. This man wasn't really interested in what was in the Books. All the fellow wanted to hear was: 'Yes you can do it.' So this Garuda is now raising him, the Acharya, to the skies, for a 'Yes' that would silence all fault-finding tongues. The motive: gold. Generosity creates its ex-act opposite; just what Naranappa said once. You shouldn't melt in pity now; you should stand firm, see what the Books say, and do accordingly.

'What do you say, the ancient sages knew past, present and future. Is it possible they didn't think about this problem, or what?'

The Acharya didn't answer and continued to read.

'Acharya-re, you once said—our Philosophy is called Ved-anta, because it's the end, the *anta*, of all thinking. Is it ever

29

possible that such Vedanta has no solution for us? Especially when—what do you say—a brahmin corpse lies untouched in the agrahara, thwarting every daily duty for a whole colony of brahmins—what do you say—they can't eat till they take care of the body—I don't mean just that—'

Praneshacharya didn't answer. Garuda was returning all the Vedanta, Purana, and logic he'd heard from him—for what? Gold. Alas for men's lives.

'Furthermore, what you said was very right. He abandoned brahminhood, but brahminhood didn't abandon him, did it? We didn't get him excommunicated, did we? What do you say—if we had really excommunicated him, he'd have become a Muslim and we'd have had to leave the unclean agrahara, what?'

The Acharya lifted his eyes and said, 'Garuda, I've decided to do just what the Books say—' and continued to read, hoping to end the conversation.

'Suppose one didn't get an answer in the Books. Not that I mean we can't get it there. Suppose we didn't. Haven't you yourself said, there's such a thing as a dharma, a rule for emergencies? Didn't you—what—once suggest that—if a man's life depended on it we could feed him even cow's flesh —such a thing wouldn't be a sin—didn't you say? What do you say—a story you told us once—Sage Vishvamitra, when the earth was famine-stricken, found hunger unbearable, and ate dog-meat, because the supreme dharma is the saving of a life?—What do you say?...'

'I understand, Garuda. Why don't you just come out and say what you have in mind?' said Praneshacharya, wearily closing his palm-leaf books.

'Nothing, nothing at all really,' said Garuda and looked at the ground. Then he abruptly prostrated himself full length before the Acharya, stood up, and said:

'Who'll get my son Shyama out of the army, Acharya-re?

30

And tell me, who but my son can do my rites when I die? So, if you'd kindly give me permission, what . . . ?'

As he said these words, Lakshmana entered and stood next to him.

Lakshmana's wife Anasuya had come home in tears that day; her sister's ornaments were now someone else's; because of that whore, Chandri, her sister had died. Her tears flowed for Naranappa too. Wasn't he, after all, her maternal uncle's son? If only Uncle were alive, if only her sister were alive, if only Garuda hadn't used black magic against our Naranappa and driven him out of his mind, would he have thrown away so much gold, would he have died like a vagabond, a homeless wretch? Would he be lying there now, rotting without last rites? These thoughts made her cry out aloud. She leaned against the wall and shed tears, saying, 'O God, O God, whatever he might have done, how can we cut the family bond that binds us?' The very next minute her eye fell on her daughter Lilavati—short, plump and round, a nose-ring in one nostril and a long vermilion mark on the brow, wearing a dwarfish braid of hair very tight—and her heart hardened again.

She asked for the tenth time, 'Did Shripati say when he was coming back?'

Lilavati said, 'I don't know.' She had married her daughter to orphan Shripati, but then her own blood-kin Naranappa had misled him and perverted him. That serpent eats its own eggs. Who knows what awful things he poured into her son-in-law's head? Shripati hardly stays home, hardly two days in a month. Roams from town to town, on the heels of Yakshagana players' troupes; keeps the company of Parijatapura boys. News had reached her through Durgabhatta's wife that he even had a prostitute or two. She knew long ago he would come to ruin; ever since she'd seen him one day sneak

31

furtively in and out of Naranappa's house, she knew he'd gone astray. Who knows what godawful things he ate and drank in that house? No one could escape falling for that woman Chandri. So Anasuya had taught her daughter a trick, just to teach her roving son-in-law a lesson: 'Don't you give in to your husband when he wants it. Knot up your thighs, like this, and sleep aloof. Teach him a lesson.' Lilavati had done exactly as she was told. When her husband came at night to embrace her, she would come crying to her mother, complaining that he pinched and bit her—and she started sleeping next to her mother.

Shripati didn't learn his lesson. Anasuya's methods didn't work with him, though these had once worked on her husband and forced him to give in to her. Shripati cut off his brahmin tuft, wore his hair in a crop, Western style, like Naranappa. He saved money and bought a flashlight. He had taken to roaming round the agrahara every evening, whistling obscenely.

Lakshmanacharya came home and fell on his bed, looking leaner than ever, wearied by heat and hunger—his frame already thinned by fevers, eyes sunk in their sockets. He seemed to be counting his days. Anasuya nagged him. 'Wasn't Naranappa my own maternal uncle's son? Sinner he may be. But if any lowcaste man is allowed to pick up his dead body, I'll die of shame. Praneshacharya is much too soft-hearted. That Garuda is clever, quite ready to gobble up the whole town. He's no milksop like you. If he should get permission to do the death-rite, all that jewelry will go to his wife Sita; she already struts about so proudly. God has pretty well taken care of their mean hearts, though—why else would their son Shyama run away and join the army? These same people say such things about Naranappa, my cousin, my uncle's son—these very people—where's the guarantee their son is keeping the faith in those army barracks? Don't

you let that man Garuda go to Praneshacharya and win over
his heart. You'd better go too. You lie here like a log and
that fellow is out there—don't I know it?'

Then she came out and carefully examined the back
and front of Garuda's house, and pushed her husband
out.

Garuda felt tremendous rage when he saw the thin Ku-
chela-like form of Lakshmana right next to him, appearing
suddenly like a bear let loose in the middle of a service for
Shiva. Lakshmana sat down, gasping, holding in his protruding heavy belly with one hand, and leaning on the ground
with the other. Garuda looked at him as if he would devour
him whole. He wanted to call him all sorts of names like
niggard of niggards, emperor of penny-pinchers, mother-
deceiver, but held them in because Praneshacharya was
sitting right there. This fellow doesn't buy a spoon of oil for
his bath, his fist is rigid as stone, this is the meanest of brahmins. Who in the agrahara doesn't know it? When his wife
nags him about an oil-bath he gets up in the morning and
walks four miles to the Konkaniman's shop. 'Hey, Kamat,
have you any fresh sesame oil? Is it any good? What does it
sell for? It isn't musty, is it? Let me see.' With such patter,
he cups his hands and gets a couple of spoons as sample,
pretends to smell it and says: 'It's all right, still a bit impure.
Tell me when you get real fresh stuff, we need a can of oil for
our house.' And smears the oil all over his head. Then he
puts his hands into the sack of red peppers, and while asking
the price, picks up a fistful and transfers it to his bag, all the
while chatting casually. From there he walks a mile to
Shenoy's shop; there he slanders Kamat's shop, and picks
up another couple of spoons of oil for his bath and for a
fresh-cooked meal. Then he forages again in someone or
other's grove, brings home some cuts of banana-leaf to dry

33

them in the sun and make leaf-cups which he will sell for a few pice. Or sells sacred thread to make a few more pice. Waits like a vulture to get invited to meals. Now his eyes are on the gold. Come what may—one must see to it that he doesn't get the loot.

Lakshmana gasped. 'Narayana, Narayana'. He wiped the sweat off his body, closed his eyes, and said, 'Acharya-re, if the Books have no objection, I've none either. Naranappa is my wife's sister's husband, isn't he, after all? If you don't mind, no one but me has the right to perform the death-rites.' And opened his eyes.

Garuda was nonplussed. How can he counter this? It was his turn.

'If it's the problem of who's qualified to perform the rite—what do you say. You can do it yourself. After all we are born as brahmins only to take on others' sins. But that gold must be submitted to the court. Or else, according to the decree at Dharmasthala, it must come to me.'

Praneshacharya felt disturbed. Even if the problem of the dead man's rites should be solved, the problem of the gold ornaments would not be easy to solve. Minute by minute his own responsibilities seemed to grow. Naranappa's challenge was growing, growing enormous like God Trivikrama who started out as a dwarf and ended up measuring the cosmos with his giant feet.

Just then the poor brahmins came over in a group, led by poor Dasacharya.

Dasacharya fondled his belly as a mother fondles a crying child. He said: 'You know I'm not well. I'll die if I miss meals. You must find a way. This is an emergency and there must be a special rule for it. Tell us if we can eat while there's a dead body in the agrahara. In a day the body will begin to stink. My house is quite close to his. This isn't good for any one. For the sake of the whole agrahara, Laksh-

34

manacharya or Garudacharya should come to some clear decision. . . .'

He stopped and looked round at everybody. What lust was to Naranappa, hunger was to Dasacharya. At this moment, hunger saved him, gave him a large heart.

'All it takes is a word from you, Acharya-re. Your word is gospel; it's like the Vedas. We don't want the gold, or anything. You tell us. Four of us will pick up the body this minute and finish the cremation rites. You can take the gold, make a crown, offer it to Lord Maruti on our behalf.'

Goodness suddenly stirred within Praneshacharya. Only Garuda and Lakshmana were crestfallen. Garuda thought hard and searched for the right thing to say. It would be sinful to contradict Dasacharya's suggestion that the gold should go to God Maruti.

'Let our Acharya do as the dharma dictates. Some people won't like it. When the Acharya searches for the answer—what do you say—it shouldn't seem wrong to the guru—what—then what'll be our fate? Nothing should hurt the good name of our Acharya also. What do you say? We shouldn't fall out of favour like the Parijatapura people, with the high-caste brahmins . . .'—said Garuda, smiling, pretending to agree with Dasacharya. Even Lakshmana, who didn't know how to sweet-talk his way out, was pleased.

'Please. Go home now, all of you. I'll find the answer even if I've to turn the whole science of dharma upside down. I'll sit up all night,' said Praneshacharya, very tired.

It was evening. He hadn't yet offered his prayers or had his dinner. Agitated, Praneshacharya walked up and down, indoors, outdoors, and back. He asked Chandri, who was in the verandah, to come in and sit inside. He lifted his ailing wife with both hands like a baby, took her to the backyard, let her pass water, brought her back to her bed and made her

35

drink her evening dose of medicine. Then he came back to the middle hall and sat there turning over and over the ancient books in the light of the kerosene lantern.

V

Shripati had gone to Shirnali the night before, to see *Jambavati's Wedding* performed by the troupe from Kelur. He didn't really know anything about Naranappa's return from Shivamogge or about his being sick in bed, or his dying. If he'd known it, he would have been grief-stricken. For Naranappa had been his one secret friend in the whole agrahara. He'd left home over a week ago. He made friends with the balladeer of the Kelur troupe, stayed with him wherever the troupe stopped, ate with them, went to their night shows, slept all day. In his spare time he'd gone to the neighbouring villages and persuaded them to invite the troupe for performances. He'd forgotten the whole world for a week happy in greetings and casual conversations. And tonight he was returning, flashlight in hand, singing loudly, in the scary forest dark. His hair was brushed back, uncut; he'd grown it long; down his neckline, because the balladeer had promised him a girl's role in next year's play. After all, his tongue had been trained by Praneshacharya, hadn't it? The balladeer had admired his pure enunciation, his clear voice. Shripati had heard enough Sanskrit and logic and ancient epics from the Acharya to give him enough culture for the ad-lib dialogues and profundities of these players of epic plays. If only he could get a part in the troupe, he could escape the brahmin dump, escape the endless funeral cakes and funeral porridge, escape all that living and dying for jackfruit curry. The thought filled Shripati with joy; so he wasn't scared any more of the dark forest. He'd also had a drink of toddy in shaman Shina's hut, and being a little high on it, didn't shiver any more at the fearful silence of the forest. Two bottles of toddy; a flashlight pouring forth brilliant light at the touch of a button to the great amazement of peasants— what ghost or demon can touch a man armed with these weapons? As he neared Durvasapura, his body warmed to the thought of the pleasures awaiting him. Who cares if his wife tightens and twines up her thighs? There was Belli. An outcaste, so what? As Naranappa would say—who cares if she's a goddess or a shaven widow? But Belli was neither. Which brahmin girl,—cheek sunken, breast withered, mouth stinking of lentil soup,—which brahmin girl was equal to Belli? Her thighs are full. When she's with him she twists like a snake coupling with another, writhing in the sands. She'd have bathed by now in water heated in mudpots outside her hut; she'd have drunk her father's sour toddy, she'd be warm and ready—like a tuned-up drum. Not utterly black-skinned, nor pale white, her body is the colour of the earth, fertile, ready for seed, warmed by an early sun. Shripati's footfall stopped dead. With pleasure, he squeezed the flash-light button, turning it on and off. He turned it around in the forest, happy like the actors in demon roles. *Ththai ththai thaka ththai ththai*: he danced to their rhythms. He tried a quick sit-down like them, rotating his knees like them, but hurt a knee and stood up. The forest was empty. Birds flapped their wings, wakened and frightened by the flashlight. He got a little more drunk with it. As he called on them, the Nine Essences of feeling presented themselves to him as to any artist—rage, disgust, terror, tender devotion, love, whichever. His fancy glided from one to the other. Now Goddess Lakshmi wakes at dawn her lord, Vishnu asleep on the serpent-coil, with her morning song:

> Wake, wake, O Narayana
> Wake, O Lord of Lakshmi
> Wa . . aa . . ke, it's morni . . ii . . ng . . .

Shripati's eyes filled and glowed with tears. Garuda, Lord Vishnu's carrier-bird, comes to wake Him up. 'Wake up, O Narayana.' Narada, messenger and sage, comes strumming on his strings to wake Him. 'Get up, O Lord of Lakshmi.' Birds and beasts, monkeys, and singing orders of supernaturals, come and beg of Him to wake up. 'O wake, it's mo . . oo . . rni . . ing!' Shripati, in a dancing measure, held his dhoti as if it were a woman's sari, and shook it, moved his neck to one side, and danced. Shina's toddy had really made him high. He should go to Naranappa's and drink some more. He remembered all the heroines. In the legends there isn't a sage who doesn't fall for some woman. That temptress Menaka, who destroyed the penance of Sage Vishvamitra. What a wench she must have been. Must have been lovelier than Chandri. It's amazing that no one's eye had fallen on Belli; she walked around everywhere in rags, picking up manure. But then it wasn't surprising either. How can brahmin eyes see anything, dimmed by looking for meals everywhere? Praneshacharya describes women again and again, talking as if to infants: 'The sage must have been thrilled, as he looked at the goddess of dawn. The Lord put these words into his mouth: "Like the thighs of a blossoming woman, pure after her monthly baths". What a bold conception, what a lovely simile!' But then, to these barren brahmins it's one more chant, one more formula for making a living. That Nagappa of Kundapura who plays king's roles, how haughtily, how seductively he speaks! 'O what bees, what blossoming *parijata* and *champak* and jasmine and scented screw-pine in this garden! O who are you, lovely woman, alone, downcast? You seem so burdened with sorrow, O who are you?' Shripati walked on, smiling. In the entire agrahara, only two people had an eye for beautiful things: Naranappa and Chandri. Chandri was utterly beautiful, beyond compare. In a hundred-mile radius, show me such a doll, and I'll say you're a man. That fellow Durgabhatta does have some good taste. But he doesn't have the guts to do more than paw at a coolie-woman's breast. Actually, the best connoisseur of them all is Praneshacharya, really one in a million. Every evening, as he reads the Puranas and expounds the stanzas, the beauty of his style is enough to make any balladeer turn green with envy. What delicate phrasing, what gentle smiles and what striking handsomeness. His tuft of hair, the caste-mark—circlet and stripe—on his forehead. Really, only he can don a gold-embroidered shawl, and it looks becoming. He's supposed to have fifteen such shawls—all won in argument and controversy in eight monasteries, against great southern pundits. But he doesn't brag about it. Poor man, his wife's a chronic invalid—no children, nothing. This man who speaks so beautifully about Kalidasa's women, does he feel any desire himself? Actually, Shripati had taken Belli at the river when she had come to get water, only after he had heard the Acharya speak of Shakuntala's beauty. He couldn't stand it any more. Belli was carrying a pitcher of water on her head, the rag on her body had slipped, and as she stood in the moonlight bouncing her breasts, the colour of earth— she'd looked like Shakuntala herself. He had then personally, carnally, enjoyed the Acharya's description.

Tonight Shripati took an inside trail and walked straight to the outcaste hutments on the hillside. In the black new-moon night he saw a hut on fire, burning away. In the light of that fire, various inky forms. He looked from a distance, listened. No one seemed too anxious to put out the fire. Baffled, he waited behind a stump. The hut, built out of bamboo frames, thatched with mats, covered with coconut fronds, burned to cinders in the dry summer heat. It was razed to the ground before his eyes. The inky silhouettes returned to their nests. Shripati stepped softly and clapped his hands a little outside Belli's hut.

Belli, her hair washed in warm water, wearing only a piece below her waist, naked above, waves of hair pouring over her back and face—came quietly out of her hut, and moved into the bushes in the distance. Shripati waited behind a tree till she disappeared, looked this way and that to make sure no one else was about, then went to the bush where Belli crouched. He turned his flashlight on and off and embraced her, panting hard.

'*Ayya*, please, not today.'

Belli had never talked like that. Shripati was amazed, but disregarded her words and undid her waist-cloth.

'I don't know what's the matter—Pilla and his woman died today—struck by a demon or something, *ayya*.'

Shripati had no use for words right now. She was naked. He pulled her down to the ground.

'Because both of them died, we left the bodies right there and fired the hut. Some kind of fever. They never opened their eyes.'

Shripati was impatient. She was saying something, was somewhere else. He had come to her with such urgent desire, here she was prating about someone croaking. She had never talked like that at such times. She had always been like ripe ears of corn bending before the falling rain.

Belli, wrapping the cloth round herself, said:

'*Ayya*, I want to tell you something. I've never seen such a thing before. Why should rats and mice come to our poor huts? Nothing there to eat. Our huts aren't like brahmin houses. Now the rats come like relatives looking for a place to stay. They fall pattering from the roof, run round and round, and die. Like folks running for life from a hut on fire, they run into the forest. I've never seen the likes of it. We must get the shaman possessed with the demon and ask him about it. Why do rats come to pariah huts and pop off? Snap! Like that! Like breaking a twig. We must ask the demon.'

40

Shripati wrapped on his dhoti again, put on his shirt, took out a pocket comb, combed his cropped hair and ran in a hurry, flashing his light. Belli was all right for sleeping with, she was no good for talk. If she opens her mouth, she talks only ghosts and demons.

Anxious to see Naranappa, he tucked his dhoti up to knee-length and ran downhill. He could drink a glass of water there, sleep there that night and go to Nagaraja's place in Parijatapura in the morning. He stood quietly before Naranappa's door and pushed it. It wasn't latched. 'He's still up,' he thought, and went in happily. He turned his flashlight on and called out, 'Naranappa, Naranappa.' No answer. There was a stench of something rotting, enough to make one sick in the stomach. He wanted to go upstairs, knock at the door of his room; he walked in the dark towards the stairs he knew so well. When he turned the corner, his bare foot swished on something soft and cold. Startled, he flashed his light on it. A dead rat, dead on its back, its legs up in the air. The flies on it buzzed in the beam of the flashlight. He ran up the steps to the room upstairs; the steps rattled under his feet. Why is Naranappa sleeping on the floor with the blanket over his head? He must have drunk till the liquor came out of his nose. Shripati smiled and pulled down the blanket and shook Naranappa, calling, 'Naranappa, Naranappa.' Like the rat, the body was cold. He pulled back his hand in a hurry and turned on his flashlight. Open-lidded, sightless eyes, turned upwards for ever. In the circle of his flashlight, flies, small insects. And a stench.

VI

Lakshmidevamma, turned sixty over ten years ago, the eldest human in the agrahara, pushed the main door with a big

41

groan and let out a long resounding belch: *Heeey!* She got down into the agrahara street, stood leaning on her staff, and belched again long and loud: *Heeey!* When she couldn't sleep, or when her mind was disturbed, she would come out at night into the street and walk up-down down-up three times, stand in front of Garudacharya's house, invoke sons and grandsons and ancestors, summon gods and goddesses for witness, throw fistfuls of curses at him, go back to her house, draw in her wooden main door with a big scratching noise and go to sleep. Especially as it got close to new moon or full moon, her cursing bouts would reach a pitch. Her door and her belch were famous in the agrahara. Both could be heard from one end to the other. Her fame had spread to the brahmin colonies in all four directions. Because she was a child-widow, they called her Lakshmidevamma the Ill-Omen. She cursed and drove away with her stick all the naughty boys, and also the brahmins who, any time they met her head-on, walked back four paces to undo the ill-luck. But no one really cared. They all called her Sour Belch. But her best known name was Half-Wit Lakshmidevamma. Her life was a Purana by itself. Married at eight, widowed at ten. Her mother-in-law and father-in-law had died when she was fifteen. The agrahara had sneered at her as the ill-starred girl. Before she was twenty her father and mother had died. And then, Garuda's father had taken custody of the little property and jewelry she had. He'd brought the woman over to his own house. That was his way always. He had managed similarly Naranappa's father's property too, saying the man wasn't bright enough to manage it himself. Lakshmidevamma had spent twenty-five years under that roof. Garuda took over when his father died. His wife pinched pennies, never fed anybody a full meal. Lakshmidevamma and she regularly had got into fights and even come to blows. Then the couple had thrown her out, pushed her into her husband's old

42

ruined house. From then on she had lived there alone. She'd taken her complaints to Praneshacharya. He'd called Garuda and counselled him. Garuda decided to give her a monthly allowance of a single rupee. So she'd become all venom towards Garuda. Praneshacharya now and then got her some rice from the brahmins. As Lakshmidevamma had got on in years, her misanthropy had risen like poison in the system.

Lakshmidevamma now stood before Garuda's house, belching long and loud, and started her abuse as usual.

'May your house be haunted; may your eyes go white; you ruiner of towns, you widow-taker, you got black magic done to Naranappa's father. Get up and come out if you've any manhood left. You ate up a poor old shaven widow's money, didn't you? Do you think you can digest it? Do you? I'll die and come back as a ghost to torment your children—I'm that sort, don't you know?'

She wheezed and belched again.

'You villain! A golden man like Naranappa became an outcaste, got himself a harlot. You fellows call yourselves brahmins, you sit there and don't want to take out a dead man's body. Where has your brahminism gone, you rascals! Don't you know you'll fall into the lowest hell reserved for outcastes and perish there? In this agrahara, in all my born days, have I seen a body kept uncremated all night? Not once. Rama, Rama, the times are rotten, rotten. Brahminism is in ruins. Why don't you shave your heads and become Muslims, why do you need to be brahmins, you!'

Ayyayyoo . . . shrieked Shripati, rushing out of Naranappa's verandah, forgetting even to close the door, leaping into the street and breaking into a run.

'Look, look, look! It's Naranappa's ghost! Ghost!' cried Half-Wit Lakshmidevamma, running from door to door, beating on it, hobbling on her stick. His heart in his mouth, Shripati crossed the stream in a hurry and ran to Parijatapura, to Nagaraja's house.

Chandri was lying on Praneshacharya's raised verandah, and she was the only one who recognized the running man as Shripati. She hadn't slept, she was hungry. She wasn't the fasting kind, not in any of her births; nor the kind that lies down alone outside a house. Ever since she left Kundapura and joined Naranappa, she had always enjoyed soft mattresses in a room perfumed by joss-sticks. Now she couldn't stand her hunger any more, so she got up and walked through the backyard to the plantain grove. She plucked a bunch of bananas left on the tree for ripening, ate them till she was full, went to the stream and drank a lot of water. She was afraid of going home—she had never seen a dead man's face. If only Naranappa's body had been properly cremated, all her love for him would have welled up in her and she would have dissolved in tears. But now her heart had nothing but fear in it. Only fear, and anxiety. If Naranappa's body didn't get the proper rituals, he could become a tormenting ghost. She had enjoyed life with him for ten years. How could she rest till he got a proper funeral? Her heart revolted. It's true, Naranappa had given up brahminhood. Ate with Muslims. She too did. But no sin will ever rub off on her. Born to a family of prostitutes, she was an exception to all rules. She was ever-auspicious, daily-wedded, the one without widowhood. How can sin defile a running river? It's good for a drink when a man's thirsty, it's good for a wash when a man's filthy, and it's good for bathing the god's images with; it says Yes to everything, never a No. Like her. Doesn't dry up, doesn't tire. Tunga, river that doesn't dry, doesn't tire.

But these brahmin women, before they bear two brats, their eyes sink, cheeks become hollow, breasts sag and fall

—not hers. Perennial Tunga, river that doesn't dry up, doesn't tire. Naranappa had guzzled at her body like a ten-year old, tearing and devouring like a gluttonous bear at a honeycomb. Sometimes he leaped like a raging striped tiger. All we need now is a proper funeral for him. Then she could go away to Kundapura and weep for him there. This can be done only by brahmin hands. It's true Naranappa had thrown out brahmin ways, but they had still clung to him. Angry, mad, strong-willed man—he had capered and somersaulted, said he would turn Muslim if they excommunicated him. But who knows what was going on inside him? She certainly didn't. Whatever his capers, he never used obscenities against Praneshacharya. Though he did talk out of turn, say rash things, he was quite afraid inside. He forgot his quarrels quickly. Someone like herself, who knew jealousy, couldn't fathom such hatred. When she joined him first, she had begged of him: 'Don't eat my cooking, don't eat meat and stuff. I'll give it up myself; if I crave for it, I'll go to the Shetti's and I'll eat my fish there, not in the agrahara.' But he hadn't listened, he wasn't the kind who would. Sheer pigheadedness. And his hysterical wife didn't have the guts to stand up to his strong will; she'd gone back to her mother's place, cursed him and died there. Who wants complications? Once the rites get done, she could offer her salutes and go home.

But something gnawed at her now. It was weird. Naranappa, who wouldn't fold his hand before a god any time, had started talking strangely as his fever rose to his brain. As coma set in, he mumbled, 'O mother! O God Ramachandra, Narayana!' Cried out, 'Rama Rama.' Holy names. Not words that come out of a sinner's or an outcaste's mouth. She hadn't qute understood what was going on deep inside him. If they don't give him a death-rite according to the Books, he'll surely become an evil spirit. She'd

45

eaten his salt, she, Chandri . . .

Everything now depended on Praneshacharya. How gentle he was, how kind. Like Lord Sri Krishna in the play, who came smiling to His devotee Draupadi, when she cried out for Him. How he glows. Poor man, he probably knew nothing of the body's pleasures, his wife lay there like a dry log, the good woman. Yet how patient he was, what a halo around him. Not even once had he raised his eyes and looked at her. Her mother used to say: prostitutes should get pregnant by such holy men. Such a man was the Acharya, he had such looks, virtues; he glowed. But one had to be lucky to be blessed by such people.

She had eaten her fill of plantains and her eyes drooped. Sleep hovered close, now far, now near. She could hear some sounds now and then in her drowsiness. Praneshacharya's wakeful pacing in the hall, reading aloud his mantras. How could she sleep when he was awake? She tried to push her sleep away. Worrying about things, she lay on the verandah, head pillowed in her forearm, shyly pulling up her knees to her belly, curled up—and slept, her sari over her face.

Every palm-leaf text had been turned over, looked into, end to end. No solutions there, nothing acceptable to his conscience. Praneshacharya was afraid of admitting that the Book of Dharma had no solution to the present dilemma. Another fear too hovered over him: wouldn't the other pundits scornfully ask, is that all you know? What would he say if they mock him—you've had the ultimate lessons, is this all your knowledge? He sat there thinking, 'Whatever one loses, one shouldn't lose one's good name, it can never be retrieved'. But he felt ashamed at the drift of his thinking. Even in this situation, thinking only of his reputation! He wished he could burn out his egotism. He opened the palm-leaves again, devotedly. Meditating for a second, he shut his eyes, picked up a single leaf and read. No, it didn't work. Closed his eyes again, picked up another leaf and read it. Nothing there, either. His wife groaned as she lay in the kitchen. He got up, leaned her to himself, and fed her two mouthfuls of lemon juice. His wife moaned, 'Why didn't I die instead of Naranappa? Why doesn't death come to me? I would like to die as an auspicious wife . . .' He made her unsay it; he made her say, 'May it only be good,' to undo her self-cursing; consoled her, came back to the hall and sat in the lantern light, distraught. If there's no answer in the ancient code-books, it's truly victory for Naranappa, and defeat for him, the Acharya. The original question was really why he hadn't helped excommunicate Naranappa all these years. It was because of Naranappa's threat to turn Muslim. By that threat, the ancient codes had already been defiled. There was a time when the brahmin's power of penance ruled the world. Then one didn't buckle under any such threat. It's because the times are getting worse such dilemmas torment us . . .

If one looks at it, was it only his threat to become a Muslim and pollute the agrahara that had kept the Acharya from excommunicating him? No, there was also compassion. The infinite compassion in his heart. As the thought flashed, Praneshacharya reproached himself, saying, 'Che! Che! that's self-deception.' That wasn't pure pity, it covered a terrible wilfulness. His wilfulness couldn't give in to Naranappa's. 'I must bring him back to the right paths; I will, by the power of my virtue, my austerities, my two fasts a week. I'll draw him to right thinking'. Such was his uncontrollable wilfulness.

The wilfulness had taken a shape all its own—the shape of a resolution to use love, compassion, austerity, to make Naranappa walk the narrow path. In such a resolve, how much was wilfulness, and how much the kindness in his bowels? His nature's main impulse seemed to be kindness. When this

47

body wilts in age, lust will leave it but not compassion. For a human, compassion is deeper-rooted than desire. If such compassion hadn't worked in him, how could he have tended an ailing wife through the years, uncomplaining, and never once falling for other women? No, no, only compassion had saved his humane brahmin nature.

Compassion, the right way of dharma, being humane— brahminhood. They all twist together into knots and torment him. The original question was, why had Naranappa gone sour, become venomous? The Books say, one gets to be a brahmin only by merit earned in many past lives. If so, why had Naranappa thrown his brahminhood into the gutter with his own two hands? It's amazing how, to the end, one works out one's nature. Praneshacharya remembered a tale from the Rigveda.

Once there was a Brahmin who was addicted to gambling. Whatever he did, he couldn't overcome his nature. The well-bred brahmins debarred him from places of sacrifice. They shooed him away, like a dog. He called upon gods and angels and wept, 'O Lord, why did you make me a gambler? Why did you give me such a vicious need? O guardians of the eight directions, give me an answer. Indra! Yama! Varuna! you gods! come and give me an answer.'

In the places of sacrifice, the other brahmins held out their offerings and called upon the gods, Indra, Yama, Varuna and the rest, to come and receive them.

But the gods went to answer the gambler's call. The brahmins had to swallow their brahminical pride and go where he, the scoundrel, was. It's hard to know the inner workings of dharma. An arch-sinner, an outcaste, reaches salvation and paradise by merely uttering the name Narayana with his dying breath. The Lord once asked his gate-keepers, Jaya and Vijaya, to choose between reaching Him in seven lives as devotees and reaching Him in just three lives as enemies, and they chose the latter. The quicker way of salvation was through conflict. For such as us, wearing away our karma like a log of sandalwood by daily worship and ritual, it takes life after life to work our salvation. The inner meanings of dharma are inscrutable. Who knows in what storms Naranappa's inmost life was involved? He leaped and played, but died in a twinkle.

If only the Lord would give him the power to know! Suddenly, like a sign from the Unknown, a thought struck him, and he thrilled to it. Early next morning after his baths etc., he should go to the Maruti temple and ask Him, 'O Son of the Wind-god, what's right in this dilemma?' His heart lightened, he paced up and down in the inner room. He remembered suddenly. 'Che! That young woman is sleeping in the verandah without even a mat.' He brought out a mat, a blanket, a pillow and called out, 'Chandri!' Chandri, who had been thinking of what her mother had said, got up with a start, and pulled her sari-end over her head. Praneshacharya felt it wasn't proper to stand in the dark like that before a woman, and so he said, 'Take this mat and pillow,' and went back. Chandri seemed to have lost the use of her tongue. Praneshacharya stopped as he crossed the threshold. In the lantern light, he saw the woman sitting embarrassed and her body was drawn-in like a bud. As he came in, another thought flashed. He came out with the jewels she had taken off her body earlier in the day, and said, 'Chandri.' She sat up quickly, anxiously.

'Look here, Chandri. Your generosity complicates the question. The brahmin has to follow whatever is right for an emergency. Keep this gold with you. Naranappa's dead. But you've your life to live.' He stood near her, lantern in hand, bent down in the light, looked kindly into her large dark eyes lifted meekly towards him and he put the gold in her hands. Then he went in.

VII

Dasacharya couldn't bear his hunger. In his distress he invoked the name of god. Narayana Narayana! Sighing loudly, he kneaded his belly, he tossed in bed. His son, unable to sleep, woke his mother up.

'Amma, it stinks, it stinks,' he said.

Dasacharya, in the distress of unbearable hunger, smelled no smells. But his wife said, 'Yes, it's true it stinks.' And tapped her husband and said, 'Look, that stench. It's summertime, the dead body has rotted. It's stinking up the whole agrahara.'

Then she heard Half-wit Lakshmidevamma cry out, 'Naranappa's ghost! Naranappa's ghost!' She screamed. She shivered. The dead man's ghost must be roaming about, spreading the stench.

In the hut, Belli couldn't sleep. She sat up. It was a dark night, she could see nothing. She came out. The hut had been fired to cremate the dead outcaste and his woman; it had burned all the way down to cinders. Sparks glimmered within the ash at each movement of the wind. In the distant bush, she saw a great many fireflies twinkling. She tiptoed softly towards them, unwrapped her piece of cloth, stood naked, pleasured by the soft wind; then carefully spread out the cloth and captured the lightning bugs, their twinkling lights; and ran back to her hut and shook them out on the floor. Twinkling and darkening, they lit the hut dimly and flew about. Belli groped for them on the floor with her hand. Her groaning father and mother, when Belli's groping hand touched them, grumbled, 'What's this bandicoot doing here?'

'Dead rats, it stinks, *isshi!*' cried Belli, as her searching hand touched a chilling-cold dead rat; she saw it in the light of the fireflies, and cried out, '*Ayya .. Ayya .. yapaa!*' She picked it up by its tail and threw it out. She cursed them. 'What's come upon these damned bastard rats to run about and die like this all over!' Then she wrapped the cloth around herself, lay on the floor and fell asleep.

Hunger beat drums in their bellies and banished sleep, giving red eyes to the brahmins. They got up in the morning, washed their faces, and came to the village-court, cursing Naranappa for the awful things now happening to the agrahara. Because of the stench indoors, children jumped about in the verandahs and backyards. The women were scared that Naranappa's ghost now roaming the streets would touch their children. So, the unwilling urchins had to be spanked, pushed in and the doors had to be shut. Never before had they shut a door in broad daylight like this. There were no sacred designs to bless and decorate the threshold, nor any sprinkling of cowdung water for the yard without them. The agrahara didn't feel that morning had dawned yet. Things looked empty, desolate. *Bikoooo!* they seemed to cry. It felt as if there was a dead body in every house, in some dark room. The brahmins sat in the village hall, their heads in their hands, not knowing what to do next.

Only Venkataramanacharya's naughty children defied their mother's orders, and stood in the backyard counting the rats leaping and tumbling from the store-room into the yard. They clapped hands and jumped about. They counted, in the style of their fathers counting measures of paddy:

> gain-O gain
> two-O two
> three-O three
> four-O four
> five-O five
> six-O six
> one-more-O one-more

When mother came down, broom in hand, to spank them, they shrieked, clapping and leaping, 'Look Ma, look, eight-O eight, nine-O nine, ten-O ten. Ten rats! Look Ma, look!'

Mother responded angrily.

'The rice you've wolfed down has gone to your head, hasn't it? What's all this business of counting filthy rats? Get in, or else I'll beat you till you have welts all over. The store-room is full of them, the filthy things. The rice and the lentils are covered with rat droppings.'

Grumbling, she drove her kids inside and shut them up. In there, a rat appeared from nowhere, and turned like a kid turning round and round himself, and fell dead on his back. The children were delighted.

Slowly the brahmins got down from their verandahs, walked towards Praneshacharya's house, holding their noses. Durgabhatta stopped everyone and said, 'What the half-wit granny said could be true, couldn't it, Acharya?'

The brahmins, quite scared in their hearts, said, 'Let's wait and see,' and walked softly to Naranappa's house. They stopped outside, gripped by fear when they saw that the big door was open. The corpse was certainly walking about as a ghost. If the correct rites are not done, he would certainly become a brahmin-demon and terrorize the whole place. Dasacharya, eyes full of tears, blamed the other brahmins.

'We're ruined by your lust for gold. Didn't I say so? That's a brahmin corpse. Unless the funeral rites are properly done, he'll become a demon. Who cares here for a poor man's words? Will it not rot in this summer heat and stink up the place? How long can one fast and not perish—with a dead body out there . . .'

Durgabhatta, raging in hunger, said, 'What sort of Madhvas are you? What sort of orthodoxy is this? You can't think of a way out on such an occasion!'

Garuda had mellowed. 'I've no objection, if Praneshacharya says Yes. What do you say—let's set aside the problem of the gold and jewelry. What. Let's first get the dead body to the cremation ground. What do you say. It's enough if Praneshacharya saves our brahminhood.'

Everyone went straight to Praneshacharya and stood humbly in the hall. The Acharya carried his wife to the backyard, waited for her to pass water, helped her wash up, gave her medicine, came out and saw the gathered brahmins. He explained to them his decision of the previous night. Garuda submitted the opinion of the entire group in a humble voice.

'Our brahminhood is really in your hands. You must save us from accusations and bad names. We may get blamed whether we take out the dead man or don't, either way. What do you say. We'll wait here for you to bring back Maruti's divine decree.'

The Acharya, starting out, said, 'You all know, don't you, that your children can eat; there's no objection.'

Wicker basket in hand, he plucked jasmine and champak flowers from the trees of the agrahara. He filled the basket with leaves of the sacred basil. After a bath in the river, he wrapped a wet cloth round himself, changed his sacred thread in preparation for this special visit to Lord Maruti. He crossed the water, walked in the woods for two miles, and came to the Maruti temple, which stood peacefully in the silence of the forest trees. He drew some water from the temple well, poured two pitcherfuls over his body to purify himself of any pollution that might have besmirched him on the way. He carried another pitcherful to the man-sized Maruti idol; removed all the old dry petals and basil leaves from the god's body, and bathed it thoroughly. Then he sat in front of the image, and uttering sacred chants for a whole hour, he rubbed sandalwood on the wet stone and made sandalpaste. He covered the idol with the fragrant paste, and adorned it with flowers and basil leaves. He meditated with eyes closed, and presented the conflicts in his mind to the lord.

'If your orders are Yes, give me the flower at your right; if you forbid the death-rite, give me the flower on the left. I'm limited, I come to you.' Thus he formed his thoughts behind closed eyes in utter devotion, and sat there gazing at Monkey-god Maruti in the light of the oil lamp.

The heat of the day was fierce, though it was hardly ten in the morning. Even in the dark temple, it was sultry and sweaty. The Acharya poured another pitcher of water over himself and sat there waiting, his body still wet. 'Till you give me an answer, I'll not rise,' he said.

When Praneshacharya left his house, Chandri, who was afraid of facing the angry brahmin faces, returned to the plantain grove. After a clean scrub in the river, she filled the lap of her sari with ripe sweet plantains, and walked on—her glossy black hair loose on her wet body, her wet sari clinging to her limbs. She now sat against a tree, at a little distance from the Maruti temple. From the distant shrine she could hear the sound of the bells rung by the Acharya. The holy sound of temple bells took her back to an experience that had moved her. Just as she was remembering her mother's words, hadn't the Acharya come close with mat and pillow, holding a lantern in the darkness, and called her 'Chandri', ever so softly? Suddenly she regretted that she was past thirty. Ten years she'd lived with Naranappa, she still hadn't had a child. If she had borne a son, he could have become a great musician; if a daughter, she could have taught her to dance, classical style. She had got everything, yet had nothing. She sat there looking at the little birds that whirred and perched on the trees.

VIII

Dasacharya was afraid he would die if he didn't eat right away. The smells of all that food cooking for the children, O to smell them on this fasting day! It was like melted butter poured into a burning fire. He spat out some of the rising spittle in his mouth, and swallowed some of it. Finally, unable to bear it any more, he got up and left. Unseen by anyone, he went into the waters of the Tunga river, bathed in the burning sun, and walked towards Parijatapura. He soon stood in the shade of Manjayya's thatched canopy. How could he ask here openly for food? In all his born days, he hadn't even touched water in the houses of these crosslined brahmins. After all, he was a brahmin who lived on ritual meals. Bad things would happen if others heard about it. Yet his legs brought him, faster than thought, to Manjayya who was eating spicy *uppittu*, made of flattened rice.

'O O O, come in, come in, Acharya. How come you brought yourself so far? Did Praneshacharya come to some decision or what? Really a pity. Unless the body is disposed of, none of you can eat, can you? Please sit down. Rest a while. Look here, bring a seat for the Acharya!' And so on, Manjayya rolled out his courtesies.

Dasacharya stood there in a trance, looking only at the *uppittu*. Manjayya looked at him kindly and said, 'Are you feeling dizzy, or something, Acharya-re, shall I get you some fruit-drink?'

Dasacharya said neither yes nor no, but squatted on the low seat. How could he open his mouth and ask him? Mustering enough courage, he started beating about the bush; Manjayya listened, eating his *uppittu*.

'I didn't really like the way our folks talked here yesterday, Manjayya.'

'Che Che Che, you shouldn't say such things,' said

Manjayya for politeness' sake.

'If you really look—how many real brahmins are there in this *kali* age, Manjayya?'

'I agree, I agree, Acharya-re. The times are rotten, it's true.'

'How are you less than any other brahmin, Manjayya, in orthodoxy and in keeping to the rules? Here you are, ready to perform the funeral rites without a pice. But Garuda and Lakshmana of our agrahara fight there like crows, over a piece of gold . . .'

'*Ayyo ayyo*, is that so?' said Manjayya, glossing over things, not interested in getting into anyone's bad books.

'Manjayya, one thing, between ourselves—everyone says Garuda's black magic ruined Naranappa. It back-fired, so his own son ran away and joined the army. Look, he even swallowed up that poor widow Lakshmidevamma's jewelry and money.'

Manjayya, though pleased, said nothing.

'I ask you, where are the real brahmins today? I've nothing against Garuda, really. Just because we get stamped and branded five ways by the guru once a year, do all our sins get burned away? I didn't like those fellows wanting you to do what they themselves won't do. Whatever you may say, Manjayya, Praneshacharya is our one true brahmin. What lustre, what ascetic penance!' he clucked.

'True, true; very true, isn't it?' agreed Manjayya, and asked, 'You've had your bath, Acharya-re?'

'O yes, I've just had a dip in the river,' he said.

'Then, eat something with us, Acharya-re.'

'I don't really mind eating in your house. But if those rascals in our agrahara hear about it, no one will invite me to a ceremony again. What can I do, Manjayya?'

Responding to the pathetic words of Dasacharya, Manjayya came close to him, secretly delighted that another of the agrahara brahmins had come to eat with him, and said softly:

'Why should I tell anyone, Acharya-re, that you ate with us? Just get up, wash your hands and feet. Look here, hey, get us some *uppittu* here . . .'

As soon as the word *uppittu* was uttered, the bowels in Dasachayra's belly turned and made loud gurgling noises. Still, he was afraid to eat cooked stuff in a Smarta house; so he suggested:

'No, no, *uppittu* doesn't really agree with me. Just a little plain flat-rice, and some milk and jaggery will do.'

Manjayya understood, was amused. He gave Dasacharya some water to wash his feet with, brought him as if in secret to the kitchen, sat him down. And himself sitting down next to him, he made him take milk, jaggery, flat-rice, plantains and honey. Dasacharya got a little intoxicated as he ate; finally Manjayya persuaded him to eat even a spoonful of *uppittu*, saying, 'Where's the harm in one spoonful?' Manjayya's wife gleefully served another four spoonfuls of it; Dasacharya rubbed his belly to the rhythm of the name of the Supreme Spirit, and didn't say No. Just for courtesy's sake, he pretended to cover his leaf with his hands, saying, 'Enough. Enough. Must leave some for you.'

IX

Chinni, instead of Belli, came that day to pick up the cow-dung. She said, 'Belli's father and mother are both sick in bed.' The brahmin women of the agrahara, too full of their own problems, didn't listen to her. But Chinni, who was picking up the manure, told her story anyway, not caring whether anyone heard it or not. 'Chowda died, his woman too died. We set fire to his hut and finished that too. Who knows if the

Demon is angry with us, who knows?' Sitadevi, Garuda's wife, stood with her hand on her waist, and worried ceaselessly about her son: what could they do if something happened to him in the army? Chinni begged, standing at a distance: ' Please, *avva*, throw a morsel for my mouth, *avva*!' Sitadevi went in, brought out some betel leaf, betelnut and a quid of tobacco, threw them at her and stood there thinking her own precious thoughts. Chinni, tucking away the tobacco and betel in her lap, said:

'*Avva*, what a lot of rats are coming out now! Like a wedding procession. Who knows what they're up to?' Then lifted her cowdung basket to her head and walked away.

When she went back, she thought she could break some tobacco and share it with Belli. As she walked to Belli's hut, she heard Belli's father and mother crying out aloud.

'Look how the fellow cries in fever. Don't know if the Demon is treading on him too,' she thought and came out calling Belli. She saw Belli sitting next to her parents, her head in her hands. Chinni was about to say, 'Look, even in the agrahara the rats are taking out a procession.' Instead she broke off a piece of tobacco and said, 'Take a bite, Sitavva gave me some.' Belli rubbed the tobacco on her palms and put it in her mouth.

'If Pilla gets the Demon on him today, we must ask about this. I'm quite scared, Chinni. What's all this, rats coming like an army to our poor pariah huts! Chowda and his wife popping off, snap! Like that! And now papa and mama trodden all over by the Demon. We must ask Him.'

'*Ayy*, you idiot—just be quiet,' said Chinni, trying to hearten Belli.

By two in the afternoon, the sun rose over the head, and burned like the angry third eye of Lord Shiva, stupefying the brahmins already half-dead with hunger. Mirages, horses of the sun, danced before their eyes as they stared at the shimmering heat of the street; they were waiting for Praneshacharya. Fear and hunger, both acute, worked in their bellies like succubi. Dissolved into formless anxiety, these brahmins' spirits hung around Praneshacharya who had gone to Lord Maruti for counsel—hung around him like bats. A dim hope: maybe they would not really have to wait another night with Naranappa's dead body. Sitadevi found a rat lying dead in the rice vessel in her store-room; she picked it up by the tail, held her nose with her sari-end, and brought it out to fling it, when a vulture swooped towards her, and glided away to perch on their roof. She screamed, 'Ayyayyo, look, look!' A vulture on the roof was an omen of death. Nothing like it had ever happened before. Garudacharya came running, took one look at the vulture and sank down. Sitadevi started weeping, 'Ayyo, what could have happened to my son!' Garuda thought at once he was being punished for refusing in his heart Dasacharya's suggestion that the gold should go to Lord Maruti. In fear, he held on to his wife's hand, came in, placed an offering before his household god, prostrated himself, and prayed: 'I've done wrong. May your gold be yours, may it be for you. Forgive me.' Then came out saying, 'Ussh! Ussh!' to the vulture, trying to chase it off his roof. The vulture had by now picked up the rat that Sitadevi had flung out and was pecking at it on the roof. The bird sat there, unafraid, defiant, like a shameless kinsman. Garudacharya lifted his head and looked into the dazzling heat above. He saw vultures, vultures, vultures in the blue blue sky reeling, gliding, spiralling circle below circle, descending. 'Look, look there!' he called out to his wife. Sitadevi came running. She shielded her eyes with her palms and looked, and she let out a long sigh: 'Usshsh' . . . As they looked on, the vulture on their roof curved his neck around like a danseuse, looked around and whirred right down to their feet to peck at and pick up another rat which had run out from the store-room to the backyard, and flew back to his perch on the roof. Both husband and wife, their life-breaths shaken up together as never before, sank down to a sitting position. Another vulture, flying far in the sky, came down to sit on Naranappa's house. He lifted his head, flapped his demon wings loudly, came to a standstill and inspected the whole agrahara with his eagle eyes. After that, more flying vultures came down to sit, two by two, two on each house, as if they had agreed upon it earlier. Some would whirr to the ground unpredictably, pick up rats in their beak and perch back on the roof to pick at their prey at leisure. The birds of prey had left their burial grounds to descend on the agrahara, as if at the Last Deluge, and everyone in the agrahara came out and gathered in the street, with their hands on their mouths. Sitadevi saw that every house had its bird of ill-omen and felt consoled; the omens weren't directed in particular at her son. The brahmins, their women and children, had stood there in unspeakable dread only for two seconds, when Durgabhatta shrieked, 'Hoo Hoo Hoo!' at the birds, trying to scare them away. In vain. All the brahmins shouted in unison—but even that didn't work.

But Dasacharya, who had just returned beaming, after filling his belly with *uppittu*, had an idea. 'Bring out the sacred gongs and beat them,' he said. The men, happy at the thought, ran into the household gods' rooms, brought out the bronze gongs and the conches. The dreadful auspicious din, like the din during the great offerings of flaming camphor, shattered the grim silence of the afternoon like grisly wardrums. For anyone who heard it in the villages five or six miles around, it created the illusion that in Durvasapura it was worship time, that they were making an offering of flaming camphor in the temple and beating the huge temple drum. The vultures looked this way and that, as if astonished;

60

then they unfurled their wings and flew, with rats in their beaks; turned into floating glimmering dots in the sky. The brahmins, tired out, uttering the holy name of Narayana, climbed their front yards, covered their noses with their upper cloths and wiped the sweat off their faces. Sitadevi and Anasuya went to their husbands and begged tearfully: 'Let the gold go to hell! Why do we need other people's property? Please take out the body and get to the rites. Naranappa's spirit is calling out these vultures.' There was not a breath of wind; the stench stood stagnant in each house, and like a bodyless ghost it troubled everyone—wretched already with heat, hunger and dread. The orthodox brahmins were distraught, as if nothing in lives to come would wash the filth of their day.

The burning sun climbed the sky. Chandri, sitting in the shade of a tree, was very tired. When her hand fumbled at the plantains in her lap, she thought of Praneshacharya in the temple, fasting and worshipping the god; she couldn't eat. She was surprised by the sound of gongs and conches in the distance. She looked around. The air was still, not a leaf was stirring. The only moving things were the gently gliding vultures in the clear blue sky. When she saw Praneshacharya pouring over his body another pitcher of water, she thought, 'All this trouble is because of me.' And it hurt her to think so. Before she knew it, her hand had peeled the plantains and put them in her mouth. 'These things don't apply to me,' she consoled herself.

Again and again the obstinate vultures came back and sat on the roofs. The brahmins came out again and again and beat their gongs, blew their conches. The battle was on till evening. But it was the brahmins who got exhausted. In spite of all their humble waiting, Praneshacharya didn't appear.

The thought of another night was unbearable. The agrahara grew dark, and the vultures vanished.

X

Praneshacharya waited desperately for the god's favour, His solution. 'Without a proper rite, the dead body is rotting; O Maruti, how long is this ordeal going to last?'—he pleaded. 'If it shouldn't be done, give me a sign, at least the flower on the left, please,' he begged. He entreated. He sang devotional love-songs to the god. He became a child, a beloved, a mother. He recalled the holy songs that blamed the Lord, listed His hundred and one faults. The man-sized Monkey-god Maruti just stood still, carrying on His palm the mountain with the life-giving herb that He carried to save the wounded hero in the epic war. Praneshacharya prostrated himself, laying the entire length of his body on the ground, and prayed. It was evening. Night fell. In the lamplight, the flower-decked Maruti didn't yield; gave neither the right flower nor the left. 'I didn't get the answer in the Books, and I didn't get it here, do I not deserve it then?'—the supplicant doubted himself. 'How can I face the people who have put their trust in me?'—he said, mortified. 'You're testing me, teasing me'—he scolded Maruti. As the darkness thickened, he realized it was the darkness of the new-moon night. He tried to persuade Maruti: 'Don't you think it's my test. Keep in mind the rotting corpse, don't forget that.' Maruti, un-hearing, unyielding, stood there, His profile turned forever towards the mountain on His palm. The Acharya suddenly remembered it was time for his wife's medicine. His legs had gone numb with all that sitting. He walked out weakly with slow steps.

As he walked a little, he heard footsteps behind him in the

62

forest dark, and he stopped. The sound of bangles. He listened. 'Who's that?' he asked. And waited.

'Me,' said Chandri, in an embarrassed low voice.

Praneshacharya felt strange standing like that all on a sudden with a woman in the dark of the forest. He searched for words. Remembering his own helplessness, overcome with sadness, he stood there murmuring, 'Maruti . . . Maruti.'

Listening to his gentle grief-stricken voice, Chandri suddenly overflowed with compassion. The poor man. Famished, distressed, he had suffered and grown so lean in a single day for me. The poor brahmin. She wanted to hold his feet and offer him her devotion. The next second, she was falling at his feet. It was pitch dark, nothing was visible. As she bent over as if overcome with grief, she didn't quite fall at his feet. Her breast touched his knee. In the vehemence of her stumbling, the buttons on her blouse caught and tore open. She leaned her head on his thigh and embraced his legs. Overwhelmed with tender feeling, filled with pity at this brahmin who had perhaps never known the pleasure of woman, helpless at her thought that there was no one but him for her in the agrahara—overcome, she wept. Praneshacharya, full of compassion, bewildered by the tight hold of a young female not his own, bent forward to bless her with his hands. His bending hand felt her hot breath, her warm tears; his hair rose in a thrill of tenderness and he caressed her loosened hair. The Sanskrit formula of blessing got stuck in his throat. As his hand played on her hair, Chandri's intensity doubled. She held his hands tightly and stood up and she pressed them to her breasts now beating away like a pair of doves.

Touching full breasts he had never touched, Praneshacharya felt faint. As in a dream, he pressed them. As the strength in his legs was ebbing, Chandri sat the Acharya down, holding him close. The Acharya's hunger, so far unconscious, suddenly raged, and he cried out like a child in distress, 'Amma!' Chandri leaned him against her breasts, took the plantains out of her lap, peeled them and fed them to him. Then she took off her sari, spread it on the ground, and lay on it hugging Praneshacharya close to her, weeping, flowing in helpless tears.

Part Two

I

It was midnight when the Acharya woke up. His head was in Chandri's lap. His cheek was pressed into her low naked belly. Chandri's fingers caressed his back, his ears, his head.

As if he had become a stranger to himself, the Acharya opened his eyes and asked himself: Where am I? How did I get here? What's this dark? Which forest is this? Who is this woman?

It felt as though he'd turned over and fallen into his childhood, lying in his mother's lap and finding rest there after great fatigue. He looked about wonderingly. A night of undying stars, spread out like a peacock's tail. The constellation of the Seven Sages. Next to the sage Agastya was Arundhati, paragon of faithful wives, twinkling shyly. Below were green grass smells, wet earth, the wild *vishnukranti* with its sky-blue flowers and the country sarsaparilla, and the smell of a woman's body-sweat. Darkness, sky, the tranquillity of standing trees. He rubbed his eyes, maybe it's all a dream. I clean forgot where I came from and where I should go from here, he thought anxiously. He said, 'Chandri', and his wakefulness was complete. In the forest, in the silence, the dark was full of secret whispers. Chirping sounds, from a bush that suddenly appeared outlined like a chariot, a formation of twinkling lightning-bugs. He gazed, he listened, till his eyes were filled with the sights, his ears with the sounds all around him, a formation of fireflies. 'Chandri', he said, touched her belly and sat up.

Chandri was afraid that Praneshacharya might scold her, despise her. There was also a hope in her that his touch might bear fruit in her body. And a gratefulness that she too might have earned merit. But she didn't say anything.

67

Praneshacharya didn't say anything for a long time. Finally he got up and said:

'Chandri, get up. Let's go. Tomorrow morning when the brahmins gather, we'll say this happened. You tell them yourself. As for my authority to decide for the agrahara, I have . . .'

Not knowing what to say, Praneshacharya stood there in confusion.

'I've lost it. If I don't have the courage to speak tomorrow you must speak out. I'm ready to do the funeral rites myself. I've no authority to tell any other brahmin to do them, that's all.' Having said the words, Praneshacharya felt all his fatigue drop from him.

They crossed the stream together. Out of embarrassment she let Praneshacharya go ahead, and when she reached the agrahara a little later, she had anxious thoughts: Why is it everything I do turns out this way? I gave the gold out of my good will, and it made nothing but trouble. And now the Acharya is in trouble, trying so hard to get the funeral rites performed right. But Chandri was a natural in pleasure, unaccustomed to self-reproach. As she walked the agrahara street in the dark she remembered—the dark forest—the standing, the bending—the giving, the taking—and it brought her only a sense of worthwhileness, like the fragrance of flowers hidden. The poor Acharya, it may not strike him the same way. Now one should not go back to his verandah and trouble him further. A great good fortune had suddenly rushed into her life. She couldn't speak of it in broad daylight before those dry brahmin folk as the Acharya asked her to, and expose him to their mercy—she couldn't do it. But then, —what was she going to do now? It wasn't right to go to the Acharya again, and she dreaded going to her dead master's house. What could she do?

After all, he'd lived with her so long—she said to herself, and plucked up courage. 'Let's go there and see, if I feel strong enough I can sleep on the outer verandah. If not I can go again to the Acharya's verandah. What else can be done in an emergency?' So arguing with herself she went straight home. She stood under the thatch and listened. Dogs barked tonight like any other night. She started climbing the steps. Her groping hand felt the open door. '*Ayyo* O God, hope no fox or dog has entered the house and done things to the body. . . .' She felt distressed, forgot her fears, went in swiftly, found by habit the box of matches in the wall-niche and lit the lantern. A horrid stench. Dead rotting rats. She was grief-stricken that she'd left the body orphaned, unprotected, the body of the man who'd antagonized the whole agrahara for her sake. She went upstairs, thinking, 'We should have burned some incense and filled the place with sweet smoke.' The dead body was reeking. The belly was swollen, the face of the dead man was grisly, disfigured. She let out a scream and ran out. Her spirit cried out: what's up there, that thing, that's not the man who loved her, no no no there's no connection. Like one possessed, she gripped the lantern and ran a mile all the way to the farmers' section. She recognized cartman Sheshappa's house by the white oxen tied up in the yard—he used to deliver eggs to their house. She went in. The oxen reacted to the unfamiliar shape, stood up, breathed out in hisses and tugged at their halters. the dogs barked. Sheshappa got up and came down. Chandri hastily described the situation and said to him, 'You must come with your ox-cart and take the dead body to the cremation ground. There's firewood in the house, we can cremate him.'

Sheshappa had woken up from a happy sleep after a swig of toddy. He panicked.

'Chandravva, that can't be done. Do you want me to go to

69

hell, meddling with a brahmin corpse? Even if you give me all eight kinds of riches, I can't. Please. If you're scared, come sleep in this poor man's house, and go home in the morning,' he said, all courtesy.

Chandri came out without a word. What was she going to do? Only one thought burned clear: it's rotting there, that thing, it's stinking there, its belly swollen. That's not her lover, Naranappa. It's neither brahmin nor shudra. A carcass. A stinking rotting carcass.

She walked straight to the Muslim section. She offered them money. She went to Ahmad Bari, the fish merchant. His late master, Naranappa, had once loaned him money to buy oxen when he was bankrupt. He remembered that, and came at once with his bullock-cart, secretly loaded both the body and the firewood into it, drove to the cremation-ground before anyone knew, kindled a flapping flaming fire in the dark night and burned it to ashes—and left, twisting his bullocks' tails, goading them with various noises to run faster. Chandri wept, came back home, collected a few of her silk saris in a bag, bundled up the cash in the box and the gold ornaments the Acharya had returned, and came out. Suppressing her desire to wake up the Acharya and touch his feet, she decided to catch the morning bus to Kundapura and walked towards the motor route in the forest path with her bundle in her hands.

II

Meanwhile, in Parijatapura, in Rich Man Manjayya's spacious terrace, several young men from four or five agraharas—Shripati, Ganesha, Ganganna, Manjunatha and others—had gathered to rehearse a play. Right in the middle was a harmonium, donated by Naranappa to their drama troupe.

When he was alive, he had to be present for every play. Without his encouragement, the Parijata Drama Group would never have been born. He was the prime mover; he added some money of his own to what the young fellows got together and bought them 'sceneries'—backdrops—from Shivamogge. He also gave them ideas about acting style. In the whole neighbourhood, he alone owned a gramophone. And had with him all the records from Hirannayya's plays. He would wind up the gramophone and play them all to his young friends. When he heard about the Congress Party here and there, he came to the village and taught the boys the new fashion of Congress uniform, of handspun knee-length shirts, loose pajamas and white caps. Now all the young fellows were in grief over his death. But they were quiet, afraid of the elders. They'd shuttered all the doors, lit *Passing Show* cigarettes. A rehearsal was on, somewhat half-heartedly. Shripati, who had a passion for dance-drama, was present, though he had no acting part. He loved anything in make-up. While the rehearsal was going on, they also consumed a small wicker tray full of spicy crisp-rice and a vessel full of hot coffee. Thinking of Naranappa now and then, eating the spiced rice and drinking the coffee, they rehearsed their play till midnight. When it ended, Nagaraja winked at Ganesha. Ganesha pinched Manjunatha who did female roles. Manjunatha passed it on to Ganganna of the Malera caste. Ganganna gave Shripati's dhoti a tug. After these secret 'in' signals, the rest of the boys were told that the rehearsal was over for the day, and packed off. When everyone was gone Nagaraja bolted the door, opened the lid of the trunk very importantly and held up two bottles of liquor. He hummed a drinking song from an old play in memory of mentor Naranappa. After that, they put the bottles in a sack; tied up the spiced rice in a banana leaf; carefully, without making a sound, glasses were packed. 'Ready?' asked Nagaraja.

71

'Ready,' said the others. One by one, as they went down the stairs, Manjunatha said, 'Hold on,' like a bus conductor and put a sliced lemon in his pocket. The young men silently closed the door behind them, and crossed the agrahara. Delighted by their own nefarious activity, they walked in the dark towards the river by the light of Shripati's torch. 'Our guru could down a whole bottle and still play the drum without missing a beat!' said Nagaraja on the way, remembering Naranappa. They came to a large sand-heap, sat on it in a circle, placing the bottle, the glasses, the rice in the centre. They felt the world contained only the five of them; the stars for witness, they wanted to shed the dwarfish Vamana natures of the agrahara and prepare to grow, with the help of liquor, into giant Trivikrama forms. The river gurgled in the silences between their words and assured them of their privacy.

As the liquor went warmly to his head, Shripati said, his voice breaking, 'Our companion, he's dead.'

'Yes, yes,' said Nagaraja, his hand reaching for the crisp rice. 'A pillar of our company broken. In this whole area, who kept time like him on the drums?'

In spite of several squeezes of lemon, Manjunatha's head was light. Trying to say something, all he could say was, 'Chandri, Chandri.'

Shripati waxed qute enthusiastic: 'Whatever anybody may say, whatever brahmins bray—I swear—what do you say?— in a hundred-mile radius is there any woman as lovely, as bright, as good, as Chandri? Take a count. If you find one, I'll give up my caste. What does it matter if she's a whore? You tell me, didn't she behave better than any wife with Naranappa? If he drank too much and vomited, she wiped up the mess. She even wiped ours up, didn't she? Anytime, even at midnight, when he woke her up she cooked and served him, all smiles. Which brahmin woman would do so much? Stupid shaven widows!' He spat out the last words.

Manjunatha uttered one of the three English words he knew: 'Yus, yus.'

'If you give Manjunatha a drink, he'll speak English,' Nagaraja laughed.

The talk turned again to girls. They measured and judged all the lowcaste women. Only Naranappa had known anything about his affair with Belli, so Shripati listened to their conversation quite calmly. It was good these fellows didn't set their eyes on Belli. Even if they did, they would be afraid to touch an untouchable. All for the best.

Shripati, uncorking the second bottle, said, 'Our best friend is lying there dead, rotting! No one to take care of his rites. And what are we doing here, having a good time?' Then he started crying. His crying fit spread contagiously to the other young men. They embraced each other.

Shripati said, 'Who are the real he-men here?'

'Me, me, me, me,' shouted all four.

Nagaraja looked at the girl-faced Manjunatha who did all the girls' roles, and said, 'Che, Che, you're our heroine, you're Sadarame, Shakuntale,' and gave him a kiss.

'If you're real men, I'll tell you something. If you agree, I'll say you're great. Okay? Naranappa was our dear friend. What have we given him in return? Let's take his body secretly and cremate it ourselves. What do you say? Get up,' said Shripati, egging them on, filling their glasses. They drank noisily; then, without a thought, they staggered and weaved across the river, guided by Shripati's flashlight. In the dark night, there was not a soul anywhere. The liquor had gone straight to their heads; they went into the agrahara, to Naranappa's door, gave it a push, and went in fearlessly. The liquor had made them insensitive to the stench. They went upstairs. Shripati beamed his flashlight all around. Where? Where? Naranappa's corpse was nowhere. All five of them suddenly feared for their lives. Nagaraja said, 'Ha,

Naranappa has become a spirit, and has walked away!' As soon as he said that, they dropped the bag of liquor bottles and all five ran for their lives.

When Half-Wit Lakshmidevamma, sleepless, opened her thunderous door and came out into the agrahara street to curse everybody, she saw them. She shrieked, 'Look, look at the demons!' And let out a long belch: *Hee. . . . eey!*

III

The brahmins, miserable that Praneshacharya did not return even late at night, shut their doors and windows tight, held their noses against the horrid stench that turned and brought their bowels up into their mouths, and tried to sleep. They tossed about on the cold floors in hunger and fear. As if from another world, there were footsteps in the night, the sound of cartwheels, the pitiful wail of Lakshmidevamma's dog-like howl and her belches. Their very life-breaths quaked, as if the agrahara had suddenly emptied itself into a desolate forest, as if the protecting gods had left them to their own devices. In house after house, children, mother and father seemed to become one shapeless mass, hugging each other and shivering in the dark. When night was over, the sun's rays descended through the holes in the rafters and brought courage in little circles of light in the dark houses. They all got up slowly, unbolted the doors and looked out. Vultures, birds of carrion. Again, the vultures, driving away the crows, sitting obstinately on the rooftops. The men tried to shoo them away, clap at them. But they didn't budge. Down-hearted, the brahmins blew their sacred conches and beat their gongs. Hearing in the dawn the auspicious sounds heard only on the twelfth day of the moon, Praneshacharya came out baffled. In a perplexity he couldn't undo, he walked in

74

and out, out and in, snapping his fingers, saying, 'What shall I do? What shall I do?' When he gave his wife her usual medicine as she lay groaning in the dining room, his hands trembled and spilled the medicine. As he held it to her lips, as he looked into his broken wife's pitted eyes, those helpless visionless symbols of his self-sacrifice and duty as a house-holder—he felt his legs twitch and double-up, as if in troubled sleep, as if in a dream he fell dizzily into bottomless nether-worlds. At the end of the beaten path of a quarter century of doctor-patient relations, of affection and compassion,—he seemed to see an abyss. He shivered in an attack of nausea. He imagined all the stinks assailing his nostrils, all issuing from that source. Like a baby monkey losing hold of his grip on the mother's body as she leaps from branch to branch, he felt he had lost hold and fallen from the rites and actions he had clutched till now.

Did he clutch this duty, this dharma, to protect this wife lying here lifeless, a pathetic beggar-woman—or did the dharma, clinging to him through the action and culture of his past, guide him hand in hand through these ways? He did not know. When he married her he was sixteen, she twelve. He had thought he should renounce the world, become a *sanyasi*, live a life of self-sacrifice. That was the ideal, the challenge, of his boyhood days. So he had married a born invalid deli-berately. He'd left her in the grateful house of her father, gone to Benares, studied to become 'the Crest-Jewel of Vedanta Philosophy,' and had come back. Here was the Lord's ordeal for him, waiting, to test him whether he had the strength to live and act by non-attachment—that was why He had given an ailing invalid wife into his hands. He would serve her, delighting in that knowledge. He had cooked for her, fed her the wheat-gruel he had himself made, done meticulously every act of daily worship for the gods, read and explicated the holy texts for the brahmins—Ramayana,

Bharata, Bhagavata, etc.—hoarded his penances like a miser his money. A hundred thousand mantras chanted and counted this month, another hundred thousand the next, a couple of hundred thousand for the eleventh day of the moon. Million by million, he counted his earnings, penances reckoned on the beads of his basil-bead rosary.

Once a Smarta pundit had gone and argued: Your idea that only men of 'Goodness' can reach salvation, isn't that only a form of hopelessness? Doesn't it mean the disappointment of a human hope, desiring a thing and not getting it? In men of 'Darkness' (he had replied) there's no desire for salvation in the first place. How can such clods feel disappointed by not getting what they don't want? No one can say, 'I'll become a "Man of Goodness";' one can only say truly 'I am a "Man of Goodness".' Only such natures crave and hunger for the Lord's grace.

'I am born with one such "Good" nature This invalid wife is the sacrificial altar for my sacrifice.' With such thoughts had he begun to cultivate his salvation. Naranappa too was a test of his 'Good' nature. Now every one of his beliefs seemed to have turned topsy-turvy, returning him to where he had started in his sixteenth year. Which is the way? Where is the path that will not lead to the brink of an abyss?

Bewildered, he lifted her as he did every day in his arms to take her for her bath, though he was bothered by the conches and gongs out in the street. When he poured the bath water over her, he noticed her sunken breasts, her bulbous nose, her short narrow braid, and they disgusted him. He felt like screaming, 'Stop it! Stop it!' to the brahmins out there blowing conches and beating gongs against the vultures. For the first time his eyes were beginning to see the beautiful and the ugly. He had not so far desired any of the beauty he'd read about in the classics. All earthly fragrance was like the flowers that go only to adorn the god's hair. All female beauty was

76

the beauty of Goddess Lakshmi, queen and servant of Lord Vishnu. All sexual enjoyment was Krishna's when he stole the bathing cowgirls' garments, and left them naked in the water. Now he wanted for himself a share of all that. He wiped the water off his wife's body, laid her on the bed he'd made, and came out again. The din of conch and gong abruptly stopped; his ears seemed to drown in a sudden depth of silent water. 'Why did I come here? Did I come looking for Chandri? But Chandri isn't here.' This bedridden woman, and that other woman who suddenly pressed his hand to her breast—what if both should leave him? For the first time, a desolation, a feeling of being orphaned, entered his inmost sense.

The brahmins, who had finally chased off the birds of prey, lifted their cadaver faces, came in a herd to climb his verandah and looked at him questioningly. When they saw the Acharya unresponsive and hesitant, they were afraid. The Acharya looked into the brahmins' eyes looking up to him for guidance, like homeless orphans; they had transferred on to his head the whole burden of their brahminhood. Looking into those eyes, the Acharya felt not only remorse, but a lightness in the thought he was now a free man, relieved of his responsibility to lead the way, relieved of all authority. 'What manner of man am I? I am just like you—a soul driven by lust and hate. Is this my first lesson in humility? Come, Chandri, tell them, relieve me of the guru's burden', he thought, and looked around. No, she wasn't there. She wasn't anywhere there. Urvashi, she had walked away. He was afraid to say openly, to say explicitly that he too had shared in Naranappa's pleasure. His hand sweated and grew cold. The desire, natural to mere mortals, to tell lies, to hide things, to think of one's own welfare, arose in him for the first time. He couldn't find the courage to shatter the respect and faith these people had placed in him. Is this pity, self-preservation, habit, inertia, sheer hypocrisy? The Sanskrit chant, learned by heart and recited daily, turned over and over in his mind: 'I am sin, my work is sin, my soul is sin, my birth is in sin.' No, no, even that is a lie. Must forget all words learned by heart, the heart must flow free like a child's. When he caressed Chandri's breast, it didn't occur to him to say, 'I am sin.' Now he was quite happy Chandri wasn't here to shame him. Thoughts after waking are different from the thoughts when one is unaware. He became aware, this life is a duplicity. Now he's really involved in the wheel of karma. To relieve this misery, he must lose awareness again and embrace her, must wake up in that misery, for absolution one must return to her. The wheel, the wheel of karma. This is the life of 'Passion'. Even if he had left desire, desire had not left him.

Troubled, unable to bring out a word, he left the seated brahmins where they were and went into the worship room. He recited God's many names—according to routine. If he didn't tell the truth—if it burns like embers poured into one's lap—he could never face Maruti again, could not tend the invalid woman with a clear heart. 'O Lord, tide me over this confusion,—has Chandri come? Will she blurt it out?' Anxious, in dread, he came out. The brahmins were still waiting. The vultures had returned to sit on the rooftops. The Acharya closed his eyes, drew a long breath, and gathered courage. But the words that came out of his mouth were: 'I'm lost. I couldn't get Maruti to say anything. I know nothing. You do whatever your hearts say.'

The brahmins were startled. Garudacharya exclaimed, 'Che, Che! That cannot be.' Dasacharya, who had some life in him today because he had eaten a bellyful the previous day, said:

'What shall we do then? Let's go to the Kaimara agrahara. Let's ask Pundit Subbannacharya there. Not that he would know what our own Acharya couldn't find. If he doesn't

78

know, we can go straight to the monastery and see the Swami. How long can we creep about in this agrahara, without food, keeping a dead body in this stench? It also gives us a chance to visit our guru. Also, the thirteenth day is a public worship day at the monastery. What do you say? We'll walk to Kaimara and change our polluted sacred threads. Won't the brahmins there offer us a meal? You shouldn't eat in the agrahara where a dead body lies uncremated, but is there any objection to eating in Kaimara? What do you say?'

All the brahmins said, 'Yes, Yes.' Lakshmanacharya remembered that Venkannacharya in Kaimara had said he would buy from him a hundred leaf-cups and a thousand dry eating-leaves. He could take those when he went there. And Garudacharya had some business with the guru. Praneshacharya felt relieved by this suggestion; a burden lifted, his fatigue vanished.

Dasacharya, very happy at his words being accepted, said: 'We'll have to leave the agrahara for at least three days. What will happen to our women and children? Let's send our families to our in-laws!'

Everyone agreed.

IV

Durgabhatta got back home, full of curses; he felt he was being dirtied by the company of these Madhva bastards, lovers of shaven widows; he got his bullock-carts ready and went away to his mother-in-law's place with his wife and children. Lakshmanacharya packed his banana leaves and leaf-cups. Dasacharya packed some puffed rice for the road, roused wife and children for their journey, packed off Lakshmidevamma also to Lakshmana's in-laws! By the time all the brahmins came to Praneshacharya's front yard, his wife had started her period. The Acharya said, 'I can't come with you now, I can't leave my bedridden wife.' The brahmins understood, and started out on the road to Kaimara hurriedly, not worrying any more about the vultures on the roofs.

When they reached Kaimara, the heat of day had cooled into evening. They bathed, changed their sacred threads, wore their sandalpaste caste-marks and gathered on Subbannacharya's verandah. The pundit said, 'You must eat first.' The brahmins, waiting just for that suggestion, poured down hot steaming rice and *saru* into their bellies till it touched the Supreme Spirit inside. Then they crowded around Subbannacharya in a state of happy languor. Subbannacharya was an astrologer: he had to know whether the time of Naranappa's dying was malignant or benign, then he could think about the proper rites. So he put on his spectacles, spread out the almanac, counted and consulted some sea-shells, and said, 'Malignant.' He shook his head, saying, 'How can I advise when Praneshacharya himself couldn't?' Dasacharya was pleased by this, and they started out again for the monastery, happy that they could get a share of the offerings of the great worship there.

'It's already dark. Stay here tonight and go early in the morning,' the Kaimara people said, and the brahmins didn't refuse their hospitality. But when they woke up early in the morning, Dasacharya lay weak in bed, running a fever. They tried to rouse him. He was in a coma.

Garudacharya explained that it might be mere indigestion, maybe he ate too much. The poorer brahmins felt sorry that the poor man would miss the great worship-service and the feast. They got up in a hurry, had a wash, ate flattened rice in yoghurt, and walked twenty miles to reach another agrahara by nightfall. They stayed and dined there that night, but when they woke up early next morning, Padmanabhacharya was down with high fever. It must be the fatigue of all that walking, they thought; and left him there. They had to walk another ten miles to reach the monastery. Whey they reached there, the big drum was sounding for noon-time worship.

V

Not a creature was visible in the agrahara except his bed-ridden menstruating wife, some crows and vultures. Praneshacharya was alone. No sounds of worship or ritual. A terrible leery silence had settled on the place. Assaulting the nostrils with the fact that seven houses away a human corpse was rotting, lodging itself in the very sources of breath was the horrible stench; with the vultures sitting on house after house, it pestered the mind, not permitting any oblivion. When he went to the gods' room, he saw to his disgust a rat reel in-auspiciously counter-clockwise, fall on its back and die. He picked it up by its tail and threw it to a vulture outside. As he came in, he was startled by the raucous cries of crows and vultures; so he came out again. He couldn't bear to lift his eyes to the deathly silent noonday heat of the sun. He shooed at the birds ineffectively and came in. Distressed by hunger, unable to bear it any longer, he gathered some plantains into the lap of his dhoti, bathed, crossed the stream, and ate them in the shade of a tree. His hunger was stilled. He remembered the darkness in which Chandri had fed him the plantains from her lap.

Did he take her then out of compassion? That is doubtful. His body's tigerish lust, taking on the form of pity and com-passion, tamed by a righteousness which had brought him this far—it could be nothing else. At the touch of Chandri's breast, the animal leaped to its natural self and bared its teeth. Naranappa's words came to his mind: 'Let's see who'll

81

win, you or me . . . go to sleep in the arms of Matsyagandhi, the fragrant fisherwoman.' He'd also told him a parable about how every act of ours reverses itself in its results. Not through Naranappa, but through him and his wilfulness, his action, the life of this agrahara must have turned topsy-turvy. He'd heard that a young lad went to the riverbank and slept with an outcaste girl there, after hearing his description of Shakuntala. The Acharya's fantasy dragged in all the untouchable girls he'd never thought of; stripped them and looked at them. Who is it? Who could it be? Belli, of course; yes, Belli. Imagining her earth-coloured breasts he had never before reckoned with, his body grew warm. He felt wretched at his fantasy. Naranappa had said mockingly: to keep your brahminhood, you must read the Vedas and holy legends without understanding, without responding to their passion. Embedded in his compassion, in his learning, was an explosive spark, which was not there in the others' stupidity. Now the tamed tiger is leaping out, baring its teeth. . . .

His hands itched to go caress Belli's breasts, thirsting for new experience. So far he didn't even live; doing only what was done, chanting the same old mantra, he had remained inexperienced. Experience is risk, assault. A thing not done before, a joining in the dark of the jungle. He'd thought experience was fulfilment of what one wanted, but now it seemed it was the unseen, the unpredicted, thrust into our life like breasts, entering it. Just as *he* had received the touch of woman, did Naranappa receive the touch of God in the dark, unbidden? Responding gently to rainfall, stirring in the soft pressure of the earth, the hard seed breaks into sprout. If one is wilful, it dries into a hard shell. Naranappa was such a wilful shell; now dead, he rots. 'Till I touched Chandri, I too was a shell, counterwill to his will. Just as naturally as the body's desires reach out to me, not leaving

82

me even when I think I have left them, why shouldn't God come and touch me, unwilled by me?'

Where is Chandri now? Did she go sit with the dead body so that he may not be troubled? How will she stand that stench? He worried. He dived into the stream and swam around. Let me, he felt, let me stay here forever, swimming in the water. He remembered his boyhood days when he used to escape his mother's overseeing eyes and run to the river. He was astonished that, after so many years, his boyhood desires had returned to him. To escape mother's suspicion, he used to lie in the sand after the swim, dry himself before he went home. Is there any pleasure equal to rolling in the sun-warmed sands after a swim in the cold water? He didn't want to go back to the agrahara. He got out on the bank and lay on the sands. In the heat of noon, the body dried quickly and the back began to burn.

Something occurred to him and he got up. Like an animal with his snout to the ground, he entered the woods where he had made love to Chandri. Even in broad daylight, it was shady and dusky there. In the bushes, it was quite dark, a humming dark. He stood at the place where his life had turned over. The weight and shape of their bodies still visible on the green grass. He sat down. Like an idiot, he pulled out blades of grass and smelled them. He had come from the death-stench in the agrahara; the smell of grass-roots smeared with wet earth held him in its power like an addiction. Like a a hen pecking at and raking the ground, he pulled at every-thing that came to his hand and smelled it. Just sitting coolly under a tree had become a fulfilment, a value. To be, just to be. To be; keen, in the heat, the cool, to the grass, the green, the flower, the pang, the heat, the shade. Putting aside both desire and value. Not leaping, when the invisible says 'Here!' To receive it gratefully. Not climbing, not reaching out, not scrambling. A small sprout of sarsaparilla touched his hand.

He pulled at it. The sarsaparilla was a firmly rooted, long creeper, and it did not yield to him. Unlike the grass, it had sunk roots into the hard ground beneath the soft topsoil. He sat up and tugged with both hands. He severed half the length of the mother root, and the sarsaparilla creeper came to his hand. He smelled it. The root had earned a fragrance, existing there, a kin knotted into the heat and the shade, sod of the earth and the space above it. The smell of it reached into him, sinking into his fivefold breath of life. He sat there, smelling it like a greedy man. The smell settled in the nostril, the sweetness entered his blood; soon the experience of fragrance passed, and he was left unsatisfied. He put aside the root and smelled the forest smells, and returned to the sarsaparilla, its smell made new. He came out of the forest and stood looking at the *vishnukranti* flowers, now become as sapphires dotting the shade—looking at them as if mere looking was wealth. Got into the stream once again and swam around. Stood in the deeper part where the water came to his chin. Fishes mobbed him, prickled at his ticklish toe-spaces, armpits and ribs. Like a ticklish boy, Praneshacharya exclaimed, 'Ahaha', and fell then swimming into the water, climbed onto the bank and stood in the sun till he was dry. He remembered it was time to give his wife her gruel, and walked quickly back to the agrahara.

All at once he saw again the crows, the vultures—felt a sudden slap on his face. When he came home, his wife's face looked hot and flushed. 'Look here, look here!' he cried to her. Had the fever risen? How can I touch a woman polluted by her menstrual blood? 'Che!', he said to himself in self-disgust, catching himself at his own hesitation; he touched her brow and drew back startled. Not knowing what to do, he put a wet cloth to her brow, he pulled her blanket aside suspiciously and examined her body. There was a swelling, a bubo on the side of her stomach. Was it the same fever that took Naranappa? He rubbed on a stone all the herbs he knew, separated her lips and poured emulsions into her mouth. None of the medicines went down her throat. 'What's this new ordeal now?' he thought, pacing up and down. The din of crows and vultures grew unbearable, the stench seemed to craze his wits. He ran into the backyard. Stood there in a dimness, not seeing the passage of time. Evening came. He was relieved to see the crows and vultures disappear, came in distraught that he had left his sick wife alone all this while. In fear, he lit the lamp and called to her. 'Look here, look here!' No answer. The silence seemed to howl. But suddenly his wife let out a shriek that left him speechless. The long raucous pitiful cry touched him in the rawest flesh, and he shivered. When the howling stopped, it was like darkness after a flash of lightning. He could not bear to be alone there. Before he knew what he was doing, he was running to Naranappa's house, calling out to Chandri. 'Chandri! Chandri!' But there was no response. He went in. It was dark. He searched in the middle room, the kitchen. No one. Just as he was about to climb the stairs, he remembered there was a corpse in there; a fear returned, as in childhood when he had been afraid to enter a dark room, fearing a goblin there; he came home running. When he touched his wife's forehead, it was cold.

He walked all the way to Kaimara in the dead of night with a lantern, and as he entered Subbannacharya's house, behind him came the four brahmins saying, 'Narayana, Narayana'; they had wet dhotis on their heads after the cremation of Dasacharya. He brought them back with him, took his wife's body to the burning ground, and she was ritually cremated before dawn. As if to himself, he murmured to the brahmins, 'There's another dead body in the agrahara waiting to be cremated. Anyway its fate will be decided at the guru's monastery. You'd better be on your way.' They left him looking on at the burning body of his wife—at the best of times no more than a small fistful, the field of his life's penance—now burning down to ash. He did not try to hold back his tears; he wept till all his weariness flowed away from him.

VI

At the monastery, the brahmins didn't want to say anything inauspicious till the holy feast was over. Silently they took the sacred water, and finished the big meal of special dishes and sweet porridge. The guru gave them all a gift, a fee, of a mere anna each. Lakshmanacharya was disappointed; grumbling at this niggardly ascetic, he tucked away the nickel in his waistcloth. 'He has no kids, no family—yet the man hangs on to money for dear life.' After the feast was over, in the main yard of the monastery the brahmins sat on the cool cement floor, and the guru sat in their midst on a chair. He was wearing an ochre robe, a rosary of basil beads, a sandal-mark on his brow. Sitting like a round doll, ruddy-cheeked, and massaging his tiny feet, he asked courtesy questions: 'Why didn't Praneshacharya come? How is he? Is he well? Why, didn't our announcement reach him?'

Garudacharya cleared his throat and submitted the entire situation.

The guru listened to everything carefully and said decisively:

'Even if he gave up brahminism, brahminism cannot leave Naranappa. Which means, the right and proper duty is to perform the death rites. But the impurity must also be cleared —therefore all his property, silver and gold must be offered to the monastery, to Lord Krishna.'

Garuda plucked up courage and wiped his face with his dhoti.

'Your Holiness, you already know about the fight between him and my father. Three hundred betel-nut trees of his grove must come to me. . . .'

Lakshmanacharya said, 'Ah', and interrupted him.

'Your Holiness, is there no justice in this matter? As you know, Naranappa's wife and my wife are sisters. . . .'

Anger appeared on the face of the round red-faced Swami.

'What kind of scoundrels are you? It's an age-old rule that all orphan property should be given over to the Lord's service. Don't you forget that! You'll have to leave the agrahara yourselves if we don't give you permission for his death rites,' he thundered.

The two brahmins confessed they had done wrong and asked forgiveness; prostrated themselves before the Swami with all the others. When they stood up, they missed Gundacharya who had come with them. They found him lying down with a high fever, in an attic of the monastery; he had eaten nothing. But they were in a hurry to finish the funeral rites. They took to the road, leaving Gundacharya behind.

The Acharya did not return to the agrahara after his wife's cremation. He thought of nothing, neither the fifteen gold-lace shawls in his box, the two hundred rupees, nor the basil-bead rosary done in gold given by the monastery.

Meaning to walk wherever his legs took him, he walked towards the east.

Part Three

I

The morning sunshine had descended into the forest in dotted patterns. Praneshacharya, dragging his feet wearily as he walked, didn't think of place and direction for a long time. For a fleeting minute he felt remorse that he didn't have the patience to wait and pick out the leftover unburned bones, the remains of his wife's body, and throw them in the stream; he had the shocking thought they might be picked and worried by dogs and foxes. But he consoled himself that he had walked away free, leaving everything behind; he had no more duties, no debts. 'I said I would walk where my legs took me, now I must walk according to that decision.' So he walked, trying to bring some balance into his mind. Whenever in the past his mind had become overactive, he would chant the names of Lord Vishnu to give it a single point and to still its streaming distractions. 'Achyuta, Ananta, Govinda.' He wanted now to do likewise. He remembered the first maxim of yoga, 'Yoga is the stilling of the waves of the mind'. 'But No!' he said to himself. 'Put aside even the consolations of recitations and God's holy names, stand alone,' he said to himself. May the mind be like the patterns of light and shade, the forms the branching trees give naturally to sunshine. Light in the sky, shadow under the trees, patterns on the ground. If, luckily, there's a spray of water—rainbows. May one's life be like that sunshine. A mere awareness, a sheer astonishment, still, floating still and self-content, like the sacred Brahmani-kite in the sky. Legs walk, eyes see, ears hear. O to be without any desire. Then one's life becomes receptive. Or else, in desire it dries to a shell, it withers, becomes a set of multiplication tables learned by rote. That Kanaka, illiterate saint—his mind was just one awareness, one wonder, That's why he came to his Master and asked: 'You want me to eat the plantain where there's no one. Where can I go, where can I do that? God is everywhere, what shall I do?' God has become to me a set of tables, learned by rote. Not an awareness, a wonder as He was to Kanaka—so no more God for me.

Once you leave God, you must leave all concern for all the debts, to ancestors, to gurus, to the gods; must stand apart from the community of men. That's why it's right, this decision to walk where the legs lead. Walk in this pathless forest like this. What about fatigue, hunger, thirst—Pranesha-charya's stream of thought stopped abruptly. He was enter-ing another cave of self-deception. Even though he had decided he would walk where the legs lead him, why had he walked all this way within earshot of those bamboo cowbells, that cowherd boy's fluting sounds? Whatever his decision, his feet still walked him close to the habitations of men. This is the limit of his world, his freedom. Can't seem to live out-side the contacts of men. Like the folktale hermit's g-string: lest mice should gnaw at the g-string, he reared a cat; for the cat's milk, he kept a cow; to look after the cow, he found a woman; and married her and ceased to be a hermit.

Praneshacharya sat under a jackfruit tree. 'I must look at this matter squarely. I must conduct my future differently, not deceive myself even one little bit. Why did I walk away after cremating my wife? The agrahara was stinking, one couldn't bear to return to it. Certainly a good reason: the intolerable stench in my nostril, the sense of pollution, cer-tainly. Then what? Why didn't I want to meet again the brahmins who were waiting for my guidance? Why?' Pra-neshacharya stretched his legs, trying to shed his fatigue, waiting for his mind to clear itself. Unseen by him, a calf came and stood beside him; lifted its face and smelled his neck and breathed on it. Praneshacharya shuddered and turned around. The friendly piteous eyes of the maturing calf moved him, feelings welled up from within. He ran his fingers on its dewlap. The calf lifted its neck, came closer and closer, offered its body to the caressing hand, its hair rising in pleasure, and began to lick his ears and cheeks with its warm rough-textured tongue. Tickled, Praneshacharya rose to his feet, and felt like playing with the calf; he put his hands under its neck and said, *uppuppuppu*. . . . The calf lifted both its legs, leaped at him, then leaped away into the sunshine and disappeared. Praneshacharya tried to remember what he was thinking. 'Yes, the question was why didn't I go back and see the brahmins?' But the mind didn't settle on it. He was hungry, he should go get some food in some nearby village. So he got up and walked, following the cowdung and the footprints of cattle. After an hour of wandering, he came to a Mari temple. Which meant it wasn't a brahmin agrahara. He went on and sat under a tree on the edge of the village.

The sun had begun to climb, it was getting hot even in the shade and he was thirsty. If some farmer saw him, he would bring some fruit and milk. A farmer, herding buffalos to the tank, did look at him from under his hand shading his eyes; came close and stood near him. His mouth was full of chewed betel leaf and betelnut, his moustache was magnificent, his head was wrapped in a check-patterned turban cloth. Praneshacharya guessed that this was really a village chief. There was comfort in finding someone unknown. Because his mouth was full of betel leaf, the farmer lifted his chin to keep the juice from dribbling, and asked with his hands where the stranger came from. If he had known he was Praneshacharya, that farmer wouldn't have stood there, his mouth full of betel, and asked discourteously the way he did. When you shed your past, your history, the world sees you as just one more brahmin. He was a little disturbed by the thought. As he didn't get a reply, the farmer went aside and spat out the quid of betel in his mouth, came back humbly, wiping the red juice from his moustache with his cloth, looked at him questioningly and asked,

'Which way is the gentleman going?'

Praneshacharya was a bit relieved that the villager had shown respect. He knew it would be inauspicious to ask a brahmin directly, 'Where are you going?' But Praneshacharya was not able to answer directly. 'O, just this way . . .' he said, waving his hand vaguely in some direction, and wiping his sweat. He felt peaceful that by god's grace the farmer didn't recognize him.

'Does the gentleman come from down the valley or what?' the villager asked curiously. Praneshacharya's mouth, unaccustomed to lying, simply said 'Ha'.

'Must be someone going for his collection.'

Praneshacharya felt like bowing his head. Look, this villager took him for a mendicant brahmin going on his rounds. All his lustre and influence lost, he really must look like a brahmin going around for his collection. The lesson of humility had begun. Better bow down, bend, he said to himself; and assented with another 'Ha'. That he could take on the shape he desired in the eyes of a stranger, seemed to extend the limits of his freedom.

The villager stood leaning against his buffalo and said, 'There's no brahmin house anywhere near here.'

'Oh?' said Praneshacharya rather indifferently.

'About ten-twelve miles from here, there's a brahmin agrahara.'

'Oh really?'

'If you go by the cart road, it's even farther. By the inner path, it's much closer.'

'Good.'

'There's a well here. I'll give you a pitcher. You can draw

some water and take a bath. I'll give you rice and lentils, you can cook it on three bricks, and eat. You must be tired, poor man. If you really want to get to the agrahara, tell me; the cartman Sheshappa is here to see a relative, his cart will go home empty. He lives near the agrahara. . . . But from what he said, I don't know if you'd want to go to that agrahara. A body is lying there dead, rotting for three nights, it seems. A brahmin corpse. *Ush* . . . Sheshappa said. By dead of night that good man's mistress came all the way to Sheshappa's house asking him to help her burn the dead body. It seems there was no rightful heir to that body. How can a dead brahmin rot like that? When Sheshappa came that way in the morning in his cart, he said there were vultures sitting on the roofs of the agrahara houses. . . .'

The villager rubbed his tobacco on his palm and sat there talking.

When Praneshacharya heard that Sheshappa was nearby, his heart missed a beat. He didn't want Sheshappa to see him in the state he was in. It would be disastrous to stay there any longer.

'If you can give me some milk and a few plantains, I'll move on,' he said looking at the villager.

'That's no trouble, sir. I'll get it for you this minute. I can't eat when a brahmin is hungry in the village; so I offered you rice, that's all. . . .'

And he left. Praneshacharya felt he was sitting on thorns. What will happen if Sheshappa should see him? He looked around, growing small in his fear. 'Why this fear in me when I've shed all things?' he asked himself, disturbed, unable to contain the rising dread within. The villager brought a cup of cold milk and a bunch of plantains, put them before the Acharya and said:

'A brahmin seems to have come to the village at a good time. Could you read me a bit of the future? I brought a bride

95

for my son, paying a hundred rupees as bride-price. But ever since she came, she's been sitting dully in a corner, possessed by some she-demon. If only you can give me something with a spell on it. . . .'

Praneshacharya reined his mind and stopped it dead, while it was about to get into action, ready to perform brahmin functions by sheer habit. 'Even if I leave everything behind, the community clings to me, asking me to fulfil duties the brahmin is born to. It isn't easy to free oneself of this. What shall I say to this villager who has brought milk and fruit to an utter stranger with such concern? Shall I tell him I've sinned and lost the merits of penance? that I am no brahmin? or just the simple truth?'

'Today I'm not in a position to use my chants. A close relative died, and I'm in a period of pollution yet,' he said, happy at the right answer occurring to him. He drank the milk and returned the cup, tied up the fruit in his cloth and stood up.

'If you walk this way about ten miles, you'll come to a place called Melige. A car-festival is on at the temple today, tomorrow and the day after. If you go there, you'll really get a good collection,' said the villager and walked on, chewing his betel and driving his buffalos on.

As he faded out of sight, Praneshacharya entered the forest again, and walked along the footpath. He was worried that his problem had become more critical. 'I'd never experienced such dread before. A fear of being discovered, of being caught. A fear that I may not be able to keep a secret from others' eyes. I lost my original fearlessness. How, why? I couldn't return to the agrahara because of fear, the fear of not being able to live in full view, in front of those brahmins. O the anxiety, I couldn't live with a lie knotted in my lap.'

As the forest silence deepened, his heart began to clear. He dragged his feet slowly as he peeled the plantains and ate

96

them. Since he saw the villager, the problem had touched deeper. One must hold it by its tuft of hair, look at it face to face. The origin of it all was a thing that had to be burned. That thing was Naranappa, who had lived kicking away at brahminism. Waiting to be burned; among all things that had to be burned some day, it stood out as a problem. Thinking that the problem belonged to the realm of the Law of Dharma, he had run to the ancient Law Books; he had run to God; but at last in the forest, in the dark . . .

He stopped. To know fully and exactly, he waited balancing his heart.

When one tries to recreate what exactly happened and how, one has the feeling of pursuing a dream.

'I was roused by the unexpected touch of her breasts, I ate the plantains she took out of the end of her sari. Hunger, weariness, and the disappointment that Lord Maruti gave no answer. That was the reason why. Undesired, as if it were God's will, the moment had arrived—that was the reason why. It was a sacred moment. Nothing before it, nothing after it. That moment brought into being what never was and then itself went out of being. Formless before, formless after. In between, the embodiment, the moment. Which means I'm absolutely not responsible for making love to her. Not responsible for that moment. But the moment altered me—why? I'm responsible now for someone who's changed—that's the present distress. Has that experience become a mere memory? And as memory is roused, I begin to desire it again. Once again I press forward to embrace Chandri.'

As desire stirred in it, the Acharya's body craved for touch. His eyes grew dim. He thought of going to Kundapura and searching out Chandri. The usually undisturbed logic of his self-examining seemed disturbed. The waves were broken. 'If I went now in search of her and enjoyed her, I would be fully responsible for my act, wouldn't I? At least then I might be released from this agony, this awareness that I turned over suddenly, unbidden. This is me, this, this is the new truth I create, the new person I make. So I can look God squarely in the eye. Now my person has lost form, has found no new form, it is like a demoniac premature foetus taken hastily out of the womb. I must examine unafraid even my belief that the moment occurred suddenly by itself, without my stir, in the darkness of the forest. It's true it occurred suddenly, I didn't go after it and get it. The outstretched hands touched the breasts—desire was born—there, there's the secret. That was the moment that decided which way to turn, No, a moment when I could have decided which way to turn. The answer is not that my body accepted it, but in the darkness my hands fumbled urgently, searched for Chandri's thighs and buttocks as I had never searched any dharma. In that moment, decisive of which way I should turn, the decision was taken to take Chandri. Even if I lost control, the responsibility to decide was still mine. Man's decision is valid only because it's possible to lose control, not because it's easy. We shape ourselves through our choices, bring form and line to this thing we call our person. Naranappa became the person he chose to be. I chose to be something else and lived by it. But suddenly I turned at some turning. I'm not free till I realize that the turning is also my act, I'm to answer for it. What happened at that turning? Dualities, conflict, rushed into my life. I hung suspended between two truths, like Trishanku. How did the ancient sages face such experiences? Without dualities, conflict? One wonders. The great sage who impregnated Matsyagandhi the fisherwoman in the boat and fathered Vyasa—did he agonize over it like me? Did Vishvamitra suffer, when he lost all the merits of penance for a woman? Could they have lived, seeing life itself as renunciation, staying with God, going beyond conflicts and opposites by living through them, taking on every changing

shape that earth carves and offers, flowing finally into form-
lessness in the ocean like a river? As for me, God never
became such an immediate urgency. If it had for anyone, it
might have for my friend Mahabala. Among all my childhood friends, only for him was God a hunger. We went
together to Kashi. He had a superb brain. He was tall, slim,
fair-skinned. There wasn't a thing beyond his grasp. He
guessed the next step even while the guru was explaining this
one. Only for him did I have a terrible jealousy, a terrible
love. The deeper friendship was not hindered in any way
because I was a Madhva and he a Smarta. While I was busy
establishing the Madhva view, only the experience of God
was important to him, nothing else was. I argued, 'Don't you
need a path to the experience of God? It's through dualism
of God and soul you reach him'. He would say, 'What do you
mean by a path? Is God's heaven a city or a village so you
can find it on a road? One should reach it from where one
stands.' He loved music more than logic or philosophy.
When he sang poet Jayadeva's song about Krishna, one was
transported to Krishna's garden. 'Southern breezes from
sandalwood mountains caress delicate vines of clove'—the
verse sprang within him. Praneshacharya's voice choked on
the memory of his dear friend. 'I've never experienced such
love of God. What happened to Mahabala? When we were
in Kashi he gradually withdrew and became distant. I didn't
understand why. I fell into great grief. My studies didn't
touch me. The fellow who was once always with me, now
evaded me and roamed about. Never quite knew why. I
never longed for anyone as I longed then for Mahabala. I
was infatuated. Some days, his sad reddish face with a black
mole on his left cheek would haunt my eyes and I'd long for
his friendship. But if I went near he would elude me on some
pretext or other. One day he suddenly vanished, stopped
coming for the lessons. I roamed the streets of Kashi looking

for him. I was distraught with the thought someone might have killed him for a human sacrifice somewhere. One day he was sitting on the front verandah of a house. I was amazed. He sat there alone, smoking a hubble-bubble. Unable to bear it, I ran to him, I pulled him by the hand. Lifting his heavy eyes, he said, "Pranesha, go your way." That's all. I pulled at him. In a fit of anger he stood up and said, "You want the truth, don't you? I've given up studies. Do you know for what I live now? Come in, I'll show you." He dragged me inside and pointed to a young woman sleeping on a mattress after her lunch. She lay there, her arms spread out. From her clothes and cosmetics I could see she was a prostitute. I was startled. I shivered in fear. Mahabala said, "Now you know, Pranesha. Don't worry about me, go now." I walked away in a daze, not knowing what to say. Then my heart hardened to stone. I came away with a vow: I will not go the way of the fallen Mahabala, I'll be his opposite. And came away. Whenever I see Naranappa I remember Mahabala, even though the two are as different as goat and elephant, worlds apart.

'Now I feel like seeing Mahabala again and asking him: "Did you change your course on your own? What experience, what need, what craving moved you this way? What would you advise me now? Did woman and pleasure bring you every satisfaction? Could that aristocratic spirit of yours be satisfied by a mere woman?"

'Aha, now I know.' Praneshacharya rose to his feet and started walking. 'Yes, that's the root of it. My disappointment with Mahabala remained with me. Unawares, I have seen Mahabala in Naranappa. To make up for my defeat there, I tried to win a victory here over Naranappa. But I was defeated, defeated—fell flat on my face. Whatever it was I fought all along, I turned into it myself. Why? Where, how, did I l ? In this search, everything gets tangled up again.

'Look at it, one is twined with the other. From Mahabala to Naranappa, from Naranappa to my wilfulness, the holy legends I recite, their effects, finally the way I lusted for Belli's breasts myself. The form I'm getting now was being forged all along, obliquely, unknown to me. I doubt now if even the moment I united with Chandri came unbidden. It must have been the moment for everything within to come out of hiding —like the rats leaping out of the store room. The agrahara comes to mind again and revives the nausea. The agrahara stands there, explicit form for what I'm facing within, an entire chapter on the verse that's me. The only thing clear to me is that I should run. Maybe go to where Chandri is. Become like Mahabala. Like him, find a clear-cut way for oneself. Escape this ambiguous Trishanku state. I must go away now, undetected, unseen by any familiar eye.'

He walked on and as he walked he sensed someone coming behind him in the forest. He felt a pair of eyes riveted on his back. He straightened up and strode on. He wanted to turn and see who it was, but he was afraid. He heard a noise, he turned. At a distance, he could see a young man taking quick steps toward him. Paneshacharya too quickened his step. Every time he turned, he found the young man quickening his. He walked faster. But the young man didn't seem to give up. Being younger he gained on him. What'll happen if he is no stranger? The young man got closer and closer. Praneshacharya's legs ached, and he had to slow down. The young man joined him. Panting for breath, he started walking alongside. Praneshacharya looked at him, curious. No one he knew.

'I am Putta, of the Maleras. Going for the car-festival at Melige. How about you?' the stranger asked, beginning the conversation himself.

Praneshacharya didn't wish to talk. Not knowing what to say, he looked into the young man's face—dark and a little withered, with beads of sweat. A very long nose gave the face the look of a strong-willed man. His close-set eyes sharpened his gaze and made one squirm under it. He had cropped his hair, wore a shirt over his dhoti. Obviously a young fellow from the town.

'I saw you from behind and thought you were someone I knew from your gait. Now I look at your face, you do look familiar . . .'

Though Putta spoke the usual words of any villager opening a conversation, Praneshacharya squirmed.

'I came from down the valley. Going for my collections,' he said, trying to close the conversation.

'Oh—oh—I know people from down the valley. Actually my father-in-law lives there. I go there often. Where exactly down the mountain?'

'Kundapura.'

'Oh—oh. Kundapura, really? Do you know Shinappayya there?'

'No,' said Praneshacharya and walked faster. But Putta, eager for talk, didn't seem to be contented with little.

'You know, Shinappayya is close to us. Good friend of my father-in-law's. He arranged for his second son to marry my wife's younger sister . . .'

'Hm . . . Hm . . .' grunted Praneshacharya as he walked on. But this creature next to him didn't give up easily. Thinking he might move on, minding his own business, Praneshacharya sat down under a tree as if utterly tired. Putta seemed quite pleased, he too sat down with a loud sigh. He took out matches and bidis from his pocket and offered a bidi to him. Praneshacharya said, 'No'. Putta lit his bidi. Praneshacharya, pretending that he was less tired already, rose to his feet and started walking again. Putta too got up and started walking. 'You know if you've someone to talk to, on the road, you forget the road. I, for one, always need someone to talk to,' said Putta, all smiles, eyeing Praneshacharya inquisitively.

II

Within a couple of hours after his wife's death-rite, and the Acharya's decision to go where his legs took him, the people of Parijatapura came to know everything—everything except that actually a Muslim cremated Naranappa's body. The young fellows of Parijatapura who had, in a brief moment of heroism, meant to perform their friend Naranappa's final rites, but had fled for their dear lives—they had sealed their lips, unable to speak of what they had seen. The thing that had disturbed Rich Manjayya was really the series of deaths occurring one after another. Naranappa first, then Dasacharya, then Praneshacharya's wife. It meant only one thing, an epidemic. Experienced in affairs as he was, in the exchanges, the markets, the law courts and offices of Shivamogge, he'd just laughed at the other brahmins' explanations. They all believed that these disasters were due to Naranappa's untimely death and the brahmins' dereliction of duty in not performing his final rites. Of course Manjayya had said unhappily, 'How awful! Dasacharya is dead! He came and ate *uppittu* here only the day before yesterday.' But he was fearful inside that he'd let that brahmin into his house. He'd had his suspicions already when they came to tell him that Naranappa died of fever and a bubo, after a trip to Shivamogge. And now he was afraid even to name the dread disease. Why overreach oneself, he felt. But when he heard that rats had been running out of the agrahara and falling dead, and carrion birds had arrived to eat them, his suspicions became certainties. His guess was correct, as surely as there are sixteen annas to a rupee. The *Tayinadu* newspaper that came yesterday, though a week old, had printed the news in a corner: 'Plague in Shivamogge'. Naranappa did bring the plague into the agrahara, and plague spreads like wildfire. Being inert all this while, bound to some blind belief and not doing the dead man's last rites—was like drawing a slab of stone over one's own head. Fools. Even he had been an idiot. Standing in the front yard, he suddenly called out, 'Fix the carts, at once!' Can't waste a minute. The plague will cross the river and come to our agrahara. It's enough if a crow or vulture brings in its beak a single plague rat and drops it—everything will be finished here.' He stood outside his house and announced in a shouting voice so that everyone could hear: 'Till I return from the city no one should go near Durvasapura.' As the leader of the agrahara, he didn't have the heart to scare them with his suspicions of plague. The bullock cart was ready. He sat against the pillow inside the curved wagon, and ordered the cartman to drive to Tirtha-halli. In his very practical brain, the decisions were well-formed already: one, to tell the municipality and get the dead body removed; two, to call in doctors and get everybody inoculated; three, to get rat exterminators and pumps, fill the ratholes with poison gas and stop them up; four, if necessary, to evacuate the people from the agrahara. For quite some time he muttered to himself like a chant—'The idiots, the idiots!'— between words of encouragement to the cartman to twist the bullocks' tails and drive the cart faster. The cart soon got on to the Tirthahalli road and moved swiftly on it.

Leaving the monastery in disappointment, Garudacharya, Lakshmanacharya and others came to the agrahara, chanting 'Hari Hari'. Padmanabhacharya lay in a high fever. When they arrived, he was in a coma. One of them had gone to the sick man's in-laws in another village to inform his wife of his condition. Another ran to the city to get a doctor. Garuda-

charya was scared. In the monastery, Gundacharya took to
bed with a fever; in Kaimara Dasacharya was sick. Here
Padmanabhacharya's tongue was hanging out. The agrahara
was in some kind of danger. In front of everyone, Lakshmana abused Garuda for preventing Naranappa's funeral
rites. But no one cared, this was no time for abuse, it was
better to hurry and finish the rites and offer to God the whole
property as penalty. Reluctantly they left the sick Padmanabhacharya behind, and started out. Garuda folded his
hands to the others and pleaded, 'Please take the monastery
doctor with you and get some medicine for Gundacharya
lying there.' On the way, no one had the courage to utter a
word. A dullness fell on them like a pall. Garuda prayed
inside himself to Maruti, 'I'll pay the penalty, please forgive
me.' They walked with a heavy heart to Kaimara, and what
did they find? Dasacharya's cremated ashes, the news of the
death of Praneshacharya's wife. They were bewildered. Their
familiar world was in a confusion. They felt they'd seen
demons in the dark. Like children they leaned on walls, tears
flowing from their eyes. The elder, Subbannacharya, tried to
console and hearten them. Garuda, after sitting dully for a
long time, said in a faint voice: 'Are the rats still dying?'
Subbannacharya asked, 'What do you mean?' 'Nothing,
vultures were sitting on our roofs,' said Garudacharya. The
elder answered, 'Finish the rites, everything will turn out
well.' 'I won't go back to the agrahara,' said Garudacharya.
The other brahmins also murmured, 'How can we do rites
to a body already decomposed?' Even four cartloads of firewood may not burn it down.' Lakshmanacharya said, 'Let's
get going.' Garudacharya said, 'I'm tired; one of you must
do it.' Subbannacharya said, 'If grown-up people like you
get scared and confused, what about the rest?' 'I just can't,'
said Garudacharya, 'Get up, get up,' urged Lakshmanacharya. 'There's no one in the agrahara. What'll happen to

the cows, the calves? No one's there to herd them to the sheds or milk them.' 'Yes, yes, true,' agreed the others. Muttering God's name, 'Hari, Hari', they started out. All along the way they chanted the praise of Raghavendra.

Belli's people sacrificed a cock to the demon and vowed they would sacrifice a sheep at the next new moon; yet both Belli's parents died the same night Praneshacharya's wife passed away. Hearing Belli's screams the neighbouring out-castes came and joined her. Near-naked black bodies sat around the hut silently and wept in the dark for half an hour. Then the dry palm-leaf-thatched hut was set on fire. In a minute the fire burned high and licked up the bodies of Belli's father and mother. Belli, who was standing there frightened, ran out of the village in the dark, thinking nothing of directions, like the rats themselves

Putta of the Maleras stuck to Praneshacharya like a sin of the past. That was his way: if you stop, he'll stop too; sit, he'll sit. Walk faster, he'll walk faster; if slower, slower. Won't leave your side. Praneshacharya was getting quite upset. He'd like to be alone, sit with his eyes shut, and think for himself—but this fellow Putta is rattling away cease-lessly. The Acharya gives him no quarter, yet he clings. Be-cause he doesn't know this is Praneshacharya, Crest-Jewel of Vedanta, etc., he is behaving as he would with a common mendicant brahmin on his beggarly rounds. He advised the Acharya it wasn't a good idea to walk barefoot so far. He said, 'You can get a hand-sewn pair of sandals in Tirthahalli for three rupees.' He asked didactically, 'What's more impor-tant, money or comfort? Look at my sandals, over a year old, haven't worn down a bit'. He pulled them off his feet and displayed them. 'I like talking,' he said. 'Come, answer me a riddle, if you can,' he challenged. Praneshacharya held his tongue, controlling his rising anger. 'A river, a boat, a man. With him, the man has a bundle of grass, a tiger, a cow. He's to cross the river with one at a time in the boat. He must see to it that the cow doesn't eat the grass, and the tiger doesn't eat the cow. He must transfer all three from this bank of the river to that. How does he do it? Let's see how sharp you are,' he said, setting out the riddle, and merrily lit his bidi. Though angry, Praneshacharya's brain was teased by the riddle. Putta walked beside him, taunting the Acharya: 'Did you get it, did you get the answer?' Praneshacharya got the answer, but he was too embarrassed to tell it. If he really solved the riddle, he'd be holding out a hand of friendship to Putta. If he didn't, Putta will think him dull-witted. It was a dilemma. Should he become a dull-witted thing in this fellow's eyes? 'Got it?' Putta asked, sucking at his bidi. Praneshacharya shook his head. Putta guffawed 'Ho ho ho!' and instantly solved the riddle. He felt immense affection for this good, not-too-clever brahmin. 'Here, another riddle,' he said. 'No, no,' said Praneshacharya. 'All right then, you better tell me one. You defeat me. Tit for Tat.' 'I don't know any,' said Praneshacharya. 'Poor fellow,' thought Putta. Casting about for conversation, Putta's tongue itched. He started a new topic, 'Acharya-re, do you know? Shyama, the actor in the Kundapura troupe—poor fellow, he died.' 'Che, poor man. I didn't know,' said the Acharya. 'Then you probably left town a long time ago,' said Putta. Praneshacharya was delighted to see the path branching in front of him. He stopped and asked Putta, 'Which way are you going?' 'This way,' he said, pointing to one path. The Acharya pointed to the other footpath and said, 'This is mine.' 'Both go to Melige. One is a little roundabout, that's all. I'm in no hurry. I'll come with you,' said Putta. He took out a chunk of brown sugar and some coconut pieces, saying 'Come, have some.' He gave some to Praneshacharya, and ate some himself. Praneshacharya was hungry, and quite grateful to Putta. Wherever he went, whatever happened, human company seemed to cling to his back like one's lot earned in a past life.

Putta moved on to more familiar terms, while he chewed coconut and hard sugar. 'You must be married, right? Who isn't? I'm asking like a fool. How many children? None at all? I'm sorry. I have two kids. I did tell you, didn't I, my wife is from Kundapura. One thing, you know. I don't know whether to laugh or cry, thinking about it. She just loves her parents. She throws tantrums every month, or every other, insisting on a visit to her mother's place. In these times, who can spend two rupees for the bus so often? You tell me. She just doesn't listen. A mother of two children, she's still childish. But then, she's really very young. My mother-in-law is a fusspot, but my father-in-law, he's large-hearted, I tell you. After all, he knows the world. My mother-in-law says at times, "What right has my son-in-law to beat my daughter?" But my father-in-law hasn't mentioned it, not once. But then my wife hasn't learned the lesson, despite the beating. She threatens to jump into the well if I don't send her home to her mother. What can I do? She's so neat, so good in every-thing else—but for this one trouble. Whether she cooks a dish, or washes a pot, she's neat. Just this one trouble. What do you say to this?'

Praneshacharya laughed, not knowing what to say. Putta too laughed. 'Understanding the way of a woman is just like tracing the track of a fish darting in the water—that's what the elders say. They know,' he said.

'That's true, quite true,' added Praneshacharya.

At last Putta's stream of words stopped. The Acharya felt, Putta must be searching for an answer to his woman's ways in some world beyond language. 'Now here's *my* riddle. I didn't look at it squarely earlier. My life's decisive moment —the moment that would describe every relation of mine,

108

with Naranappa, with Mahabala, with my wife, with the other brahmins, with the entire dharma I leaned on—it was born without my stir. I suddenly turned in the dark of the forest. But, my dilemma, my decision, my problem wasn't just mine, it included the entire agrahara. This is the root of the difficulty, the anxiety, the double-bind of dharma. When the question of Naranappa's death-rites came up, I didn't try to solve it for myself. I depended on God, on the old Law Books. Isn't this precisely why we have created the Books? Because there's this deep relation between our decisions and the whole community. In every act we involve our fore-fathers, our gurus, our gods, our fellow humans. Hence this conflict. Did I feel such conflict when I lay with Chandri? Did I decide it after pouring and measuring and weighing? Now it's become dusky, unclear. That decision, that act gouged me out of my past world, the world of the brahmins, from my wife's existence, my very faith. The consequence, I'm shaking in the wind like a piece of string.

'Is there any release from it?'

Putta said, 'Acharya-re!'

'What's it?'

'Would you like some coconut and jaggery?'

'Give me some.'

Putta gave him some more coconut and jaggery and said, 'It's hard to pass the time on the road, right? If you're getting bored, I'll tell you another riddle. Solve it. One plays, one runs, one stands and stares. What is it? Tell me.' Then he lit another bidi.

'Therefore the root of all my anxiety is because I slept with Chandri as in a dream. Hence the present ambiguity, this Trishanku-state. I'll be free from it only through a free deli-berate wide-awake fully-willed act. Otherwise, a piece of string in the wind, a cloud taking on shapes according to the wind. I've become a mere thing. By an act of will I'll become

human again. I'll become responsible for myself. That is . . .
that is . . . I'll give up this decision to go where the legs take
me, I'll catch a bus to Kundapura and live with Chandri. I'll
then end all my troubles. I'll remake myself in full wakefulness . . .'

'Did you get it?' asked Putta, laughing.

'The fish plays, the water runs, the stone stands and stares,'
said Praneshacharya.

'Great! You win. Do you know what they call me at
home? Riddleman Putta is what they call me. I'll give you a
new riddle for every mile,' he said, and threw away the bidi
stub.

By the time Garuda, Lakshmana and the others reached
Durvasapura walking all the way in the sun, the sun was
going down. They entered the agrahara hesitantly, but they
were relieved to see no vultures sitting on the rooftops.
Lakshmanacharya said softly, 'I'll go look at what's happened to my cattle, you go on.' Garudacharya got angry and
scowled, 'The death-rite had better be your first concern.
After that, your household affairs!' Lakshmanacharya didn't
dare to talk back. Everyone came to Praneshacharya's house.
Everyone felt, 'Poor man, we must offer him sympathies.'
But when they called, there was only the smell of dead rats.
After that, no one had the courage to enter even his own
house. When they came to the main street, a stupor came
over them. It had a dead, haunted look. They huddled
together and thought of what they should do next. 'The
death-rite,' said one. But no one had the courage to enter
Naranappa's house and take a look at a rotted body, probably grotesque and fearful. Garudacharya thought of something: 'Praneshacharya must have gone to the river, or somewhere. Let's wait for him.' Lakshmanacharya said, 'No time
to lose, let's at least begin preparations for the cremation.'

110

'Firewood,' one said. 'Must cut down a mango tree,' said another. 'How will a rotting body burn in wet green firewood,' said still another. Lakshmanacharya said, 'Well, we can burn him in wood from his own house.' Garuda taunted: 'No one asked you anyway for firewood from your house.' But when they went round to Naranappa's backyard, there was not enough firewood there. They called out, 'Chandri! Chandri!' There was no answer. 'Probably ran away to Kundapura, after ruining the entire village, the Mari!' muttered the brahmins. 'What else can we do? Everyone should bring a bundle of firewood from his house to the cremation ground. Everyone,' ordered Garudacharya. Everyone agreed and carried on his head a bundle to the cremation ground two miles away. When they returned to the agrahara, there was still no sign of Praneshacharya. 'The body,' said one. 'Let Praneshacharya come,' said Garuda. 'All right,' said Lakshmanacharya. Everyone was afraid to go look inside. Garuda said, 'Let's not be rash. It isn't right to do anything without asking Praneshacharya.' The other brahmins meanwhile said, 'Let's get things ready and wait.' They kindled a fire in a clay pitcher outside Naranappa's house, brought bamboos, started making a stretcher for the body, and waited—for Praneshacharya.

It was about three in the afternoon when Praneshacharya reached the Melige tank with Putta. They had walked on the big road meant for carts; their bodies were covered with red dust. When he climbed down into the tank to wash his hands and feet, Putta said, 'Look, I talked so much, but never told you anything of my own affairs.' As he washed his face, the Acharya felt a twinge of fear that someone in Melige might recognize him. He was disturbed at the renewal of fear. But one consolation: all the Melige brahmins were Smartas, therefore strangers. Who will really attend to him in the

111

bustle of the festivals? Anyway, where's the occasion for fear once he has truly decided? Yet fear is natural. But why, if there's no reason for it? One must look for its roots. Must pull it out from the roots and destroy it. How fearlessly, how royally Naranappa lived with Chandri in the heart of the agrahara! Even if he should join Chandri, he'll probably cover his face, who knows? What sort of existence is this!

'You must be wondering why I'm prattling so much. You must have thought "What a leech!" I'll tell you why. Though you don't talk much, you too need people, conversation. You're a meek person, quite a suffering type,' said Putta, wiping the water off his face. 'Am I right or wrong, you tell me. I can tell from the face, who's what type. Why should I hide anything? I hope you didn't get the impression I'm a low-class fellow. I told you I'm a Malera, didn't I? My father was a high-class brahmin. He took care of my mother whom he lived with, better than his lawfully wedded wife. He even performed a sacred-thread ceremony for me. Look, if you wish,' he said, pulling out his sacred thread from under his shirt. 'Therefore, all my buddies are brahmin boys. Let's go now,' he said. As he climbed the bund of the tank into the street, he laughed and said, 'I'm exactly what people call me. One of my names is Riddleman Putta, another is Prattling Putta. On the whole, I like people.'

The bustle of the festival had made Melige very colourful. The temple chariot stood in the middle of town, its pinnacle adorned with zodiac pictures of virgo, scorpio, gemini and others. All along the road, two heavy ropes hung from the chariot. The devotees had pulled the chariot halfway from its shed and left it there for offerings of coconut and fruit. A young brahmin took the devotee's coconut and fruit offerings up and down a ladder to the priest who had already gone up and taken his seat inside the chariot. All around was a big crowd, waiting with the offerings. Praneshacharya scanned the crowd anxiously lest there should be some acquaintance who would recognize him. The crowd was so thick that, if you scattered a handful of sesame, not a seed would fall to the ground. Through such a milling crowd, Putta led Praneshacharya by the hand to a shop, and bought coconuts and bananas to offer to the god. 'Let the crowd thin a bit, we'll offer our worship later. Let's walk around. Come, Acharya-re,' he suggested. When they came out of the crowd there was a noise of reed-pipes everywhere. Every village boy's mouth held a pipe with a different noise. Pipes bought with small change wrested from the parents after much nagging. Also the smells of burning camphor and joss-sticks. The smell of new clothes. The song of the balloon-seller. In one corner was the Bombay Box. If you give the man a coin, he dances, and drums on a box with jingling anklets tied to it, and shows you pictures through a hole. 'Look at Delhi City, look at the Eighteen Courts, look at the Bangalore bazaar, look at the Mysore rajah! Ahaa, take a look at the rajah holding court, look at the god of Tirupati! Aha, look at the Bombay concubine, aha, look at the Bombay concubine, look, look!' The sound of dancing anklets stops. He shouts: 'The Bombay Box, the Box! Just one little coin, just one!' Putta couldn't bear to walk on without looking in. 'Acharya-re, I must look,' he said. 'Yes, do,' said Praneshacharya. 'Don't go away and leave me behind. Just stay here,' said Putta, as he pulled the black curtain of the box over his head and sat there looking into the peepshow. The Acharya toyed with the idea of leaving him there and walking off. He thought, 'Poor fellow, can't do that to him. Yet he gives me no peace, I must be alone now'. So he walked away. After a few paces, he heard a voice call, 'Acharya-re!' He turned, it was Putta. 'I was really afraid you'd left me behind and walked off. But that Bombay Box man showed me the way you went. Let's go.' Praneshacharya felt like scratching him-

113

self blue all over in sheer exasperation. Should he scold him? But how can one hurt a human being holding out his hand in friendship without one's bidding or asking? Just bear it, he said to himself. 'Aha, look there,' said Putta. An acrobat show was in progress. A shapely serpentine woman, all curves, had spread-eagled her hands and legs, swaying, balancing herself on her bare belly at the end of a bamboo pole. The acrobat gypsy beat a drum. The next minute the girl on the bamboo had slid down to the ground to dance. The crowd threw copper coins. Putta too threw a coin. As they neared the temple, writhing on the ground on either side were beggars begging, beggars with stumps for hands or legs, blind men, people with two holes in place of a nose, cripples of every kind. Putta threw a coin to the most attractive of the cripples. Further on, he bought a yard of ribbon for his wife's hair from a mobile shop with multi-coloured ribbons hung in a maypole. 'She loves these,' he said. He bought two coloured pipes for his kids, blew on them, and said, 'Let's go.' Praneshacharya felt like a hovering demon, a rootless object in the hustle and noise. As soon as Putta saw a sodawater shop he said, 'Come, let's have an orange drink.' Praneshacharya declined, 'No, I don't drink those things.' Putta stood in the thatched sodawater shop of a Konkani man, carefully examined a bottle of red liquid and said, 'A bottle of this for me.' The shop was full of village women, shyly drinking soda-pop from the sweet-smelling bottles. Farmers, children. Their heads, oiled and combed sleek. Knots of flowers in their hair. New saris on the women. New shirts on the farmers. The squeak and gurgle of the sodawater as they push down the glass marbles in the soda bottles; the belch that comes up the throat after a drink of the sweet-coloured aerated waters—the whole thing was a matter of expectation, experience, contentment. Of the many pleasures of a temple festival, this too was one. Everyone thinks of it early and earmarks enough money for it. Praneshacharya stood outside this world of ordinary pleasures and looked at the gathered crowd. Putta belched with a sudden snort and his face blossomed. 'Let's go.' he said. 'But you didn't drink anything!'

In all this bustle and busyness, amid noises of balloons and pipes, the soda-pop and the sweetmeats, the peal of temple bells, the gorgeous spectacle of women's bangle shops, Praneshacharya walked as one entranced, following Putta. Purposeful eyes everywhere, engaged in things. His eyes, the only disengaged ones, incapable of involvement in anything. Putta was right. 'Even my meeting him here must have been destined. To fulfil my resolution I should be capable of his involvement in living. Chandri's too is the same world. But I am neither here, nor there. I am caught in this play of opposites.' A smell of coffee and spiced *dose* assailed his nostrils. Putta stopped. The Acharya too stopped.

'Come along. Let's drink a cup of coffee,' said Putta.

'Not for me,' said Praneshacharya.

'This is a brahmin restaurant. They've brought it along all the way from Tirthahalli just for the festival. It won't pollute you. There's a special place inside for orthodox brahmins like you.'

'No, I don't want any coffee.'

'That won't do. Come. I have to buy you some coffee ' said Putta, and dragged him in by the hand. Praneshacharya squatted on a low seat unwillingly. He looked around timidly, fearing the presence of some familiar person. If someone sees the Crest-Jewel of Vedanta Philosophy drinking a cup of polluted restaurant coffee . . . '*Thuth*, I must first rid myself of such fears,' he cursed himself. Putta stood a little further off, respecting the Acharya's brahminhood. 'Two special coffees,' he said to the waiter standing in front of him. He paid two annas, drank the tumbler of coffee, cursing it.

'Awful coffee at these festivals.' Praneshacharya was quite thirsty; he even liked his coffee. With a new access of spirit, he came out. Putta said, 'Why don't you go and eat in the temple? They serve festival meals for brahmins till six o'clock today.' Praneshacharya hadn't had a meal for days; he felt a craving to eat a hot meal of rice and *saru*. But at once he remembered, the mourning period for his wife's death was not over yet. One couldn't just enter a holy temple and eat there, one would pollute the temple; and as people say, the festival chariot will not move an inch. But didn't Naranappa manage even to eat the holy fish in the Ganapati tank and get away with it? He would never have the courage to defy brahmin practice as Naranappa did. His mind mocked: 'What price your resolve to join Chandri and live with her? If you must, do it fully; if you let go, let go utterly. That's the only way to go beyond the play of opposites, that's the way of liberation from fear. Look, how Mahabala willed and acted.'

'Wait a bit, Acharya-re. Look there,' said Putta. At a distance on a hill was a group of lowcaste folk standing in some kind of trance. 'Come, let's go there. I'm sure it's a cock-fight.' Praneshacharya's heart missed a beat. Yet he walked with Putta, troubled by a sense of fate. Standing at a little distance away from the group, he looked on. The smell of cheap toddy made him gag a little. The people sat on their heels watching two roosters snapping at each other with knives tied to their legs, leaping at each other, flapping their wings. People squatted on their toes all around the fighting roosters, mouths gaping. Praneshacharya had never seen such concentration, such sharp cruel looks. All their five vital breaths seemed to converge in the eyes of those squatting people. And then, the two roosters: a swirl of wings, four wings, four knives. Kokk, kokk, kokk, kokk. All around them, forty, fifty eyes. Red-combed roosters, flashing knives. The sun, flash, flash. Flicker. Glint. Spark as from flintstone.

Ah, what skill. One of them struck, struck, and struck. Swooped and sat on top of the other. Praneshacharya was in a panic. He had abruptly dropped into a demoniac world. He sat down, in utter fear: if in that nether-world where he decided to live with Chandri, if in that depth of darkness, in that cave, if the cruel engagement glinting in the eyes of these entranced creatures is just a part of that world, a brahmin like him will wilt. The two masters were making throaty sounds to egg their roosters on, and the sounds didn't seem to issue from human throats. It became clear that he didn't have the skills to live in this world of sharp and cruel feelings. One part of lust is tenderness, the other part a demoniac will. Cowardice returned, the cowardice he had felt the day Naranappa had defied him, when his whole person seemed to shrink before that arrogance. The men forcibly pulled the fighting cocks apart, put stitches on the bloody wounds and set them up again for the fight. Meanwhile, Putta who was looking on with enthusiasm, had wagered with a stranger. 'That rooster is mine,' he said, 'if he wins, two annas.' The stranger said, 'If mine wins, four annas.' Putta said, 'Eight annas.' The other man said, 'Ten annas.' Putta said, 'Twelve annas.' 'All right, let's see,' said the other. Praneshacharya waited anxiously. What shall we do if this callow youth should lose all his money? To his amazement, it was Putta who won. Then Putta got up to leave. The man who had lost said, 'Another bet.' Putta said, 'No.' The other man, who was drunk, got up to beat him. Praneshacharya held out his hand. Seeing a brahmin in front of him, the man gulped down his anger. The others started lowering on them, saying, 'What's going on? What it is?' Before anything could happen, Praneshacharya dragged Putta out of the crowd and led him away.

Putta didn't seem to be bothered; he had won twelve annas. He was beaming. Praneshacharya was filled suddenly with a fatherly affection for Putta. If I'd a son I could have brought him up lovingly, he thought.

'Now, Putta, let me go my way,' said Praneshacharya, trying to close off his feelings of friendship.

Putta's face fell. He asked, 'Which way do you go?' The Acharya searched suspiciously for some reason why this fellow might want to hang on.

'Somewhere. I'm not sure yet,' he said.

'Then I'll walk with you some distance. You can at least eat a meal at the temple,' insisted Putta.

Praneshacharya thought all this was getting to be a nuisance.

'I've got to see a goldsmith,' he said.

'Why?' asked Putta, not giving up.

'I've to sell a piece of gold.'

'Why do you have to do that? If you don't have enough money on you, I'll loan you twelve annas. You can return it to me sometime.'

Praneshacharya racked his brains for a way to release himself from this man. This man's sympathies were like creepers that tangle up your feet.

'No, Putta. The money I need isn't a small amount. I've to catch the Kundapura bus. And there are other expenses,' said Praneshacharya, unable to release himself from Putta's hold.

'O, is that so? Come then, I know a goldsmith here. What do you want to sell?'

'The ring on my sacred thread,' said Praneshacharya, unable to evade him.

'Let me see it,' said Putta, stretching out his hand. Praneshacharya untied the ring on his sacred thread and handed it to him. Putta held it in his hand, examined it, and said, 'Don't you accept anything less than fifteen rupees.' Then they entered a *keri* and went to a goldsmith's house. The goldsmith was sitting before a wooden box, filing away at a ring. He straightened his silver-rimmed glasses and asked, 'What do you want?' Then he recognized Putta, and spoke words of courtesy: 'What's happening here, our Puttayya's feet have brought him all the way here?' The ring was handed over. The goldsmith weighed it in his balance with little red seeds for weights, rubbed it on a touchstone, and said, 'Ten rupees.' Putta said, 'If it's less than fifteen rupees, let's not even talk about it.' The Acharya was disturbed by such business talk. The goldsmith said, 'The price of gold has come down.' 'I don't know about all that. Can you give us fifteen rupees or not?' asked Putta. Then he looked at the Acharya and shot up his eyebrows as if to say, 'See how I do business, and admire it.' But the Acharya, trying to put an end to the argument, said, 'If it's ten rupees, then ten it is. That'll do for expenses.' Putta felt let down. The goldsmith's face beamed. He counted out ten rupees and folded his hands in farewell. 'That was a help,' said Praneshacharya, and came out.

As soon as they came out Putta started nagging—almost like a lawfully wedded wife: 'What's the matter with you? Here I try to be useful to you and you make *me* lose face. He'll never value my word any more now. Of course I could say "Okay, it's you who lost five rupees down the drain!" But look, in this iron age of *kali*, you can't be that dumb and survive. Haven't you heard, goldsmiths will cheat even on their sisters' gold?'

'I needed money desperately. I was rash. Forgive me,' said Praneshacharya meekly, not wishing to hurt Putta. Putta softened and said,

'I knew, the minute I looked at you. You've a very simple soul. You shouldn't be sent out alone anywhere. I'll put you on the bus personally and then go back. Now you'd better do as I tell you. I've to go see someone. You come with me. After that you can go eat at the temple, there's plenty of time, they serve food till evening to line after line of guests.

119

You can sleep somewhere here tonight. In the morning we can walk to Tirthahalli, it's only five miles. There's a bus from there to Agumbe. If you go straight down the mountain in a taxi, you can catch the bus to Kundapura.'

'All right,' said the Acharya, tucking into his waist the money, the fare for Kundapura which he had got by selling the ring. Putta warned, 'Careful, that's money.'

The Acharya thought, 'It shouldn't be hard to give this fellow the slip when they get to the temple feast. Here is Putta, willing to involve himself in another's life for no reason at all. Who knows, what debts from what past life are being cleared this way? There seems to be no escaping this man's company. A creeper winding around one's feet. Who dare say one's life is one's own?'

'Come this way,' said Putta, and led him through the crowded temple road to a narrow alley. They walked till they came to a deserted place. There was a small stream; across it was a bamboo bridge-piece. Crossing a fence, they came to a wet crop field. As he walked on the edges of it, Praneshacharya remembered the cock-fight. How one rooster trod on another, what excitement of wing and feather! How one mastered the other, tearing it, getting into it, deeper, deeper. The knives glinting sharply in the sunshine. Then those eyes. The smell of country liquor. Even when pulled apart, laid on their backs, their wounds stitched, the roosters were pressing forward, crying kokk, kokk, throbbing. A demon world of pressing need, revenge, greed. 'I was there like a futile ghost. Panic-stricken. I tried wilfully to change and move into that world. And there was that acrobat gypsy girl. Swinging in her exercises in the sky, at the end of a bamboo pole, wearing body-tight clothes, showing off. She glided down suddenly. She danced. The sodawater bottles, with marbles in their necks squeaking when squeezed; the coloured liquids, the abrupt belches, desire, experience, satisfaction.

Those purposive eyes. Eyes engaged in things: in the midst of multi-coloured ribbons, balloons, around the pinnacle of the temple chariot, eyes everywhere, behind my back, in front, on either side. Eyes all around—the wings—the knives—the beaks—the talons. Immersed. The oneness, the monism, of desire and fulfilment. That art Thou.

'I dread it. It's the dread of being transformed from ghost to demon.'

Putta lit up a bidi and asked laughingly, in mischief, 'Do you know where we are going?'

Praneshacharya shook his head.

'My good sir, I like your ways. You really will go any-where, you ask no questions. I'm also a little like that. I once went with a friend of mine just like this, all the way to Shivamogge. My father-in-law complains, "Wherever Putta goes, there he stays put. O Putta? Our Putta: if you let him go, you'll lose him; but find him, he'll never leave you," he says.'

'You said you've to see someone, didn't you?'

'Acharya-re, please address me in the singular. It's not good for my longevity to be addressed in the plural by an elder like you.'

'All right.'

'There's a grove near here. There, that one. A woman we know stays there, running it as a tenant. She's all alone, quite a courageous woman. Really a beautiful woman; you've to wash your hands clean to touch her, so neat. Distant relative of mine. She's very respectful to orthodox brahmins like you. Let's say hello to her for a minute and then we'll leave. If I don't look her up, she'll say, "I heard you were in town, Putta, you didn't even show your face. Didn't inquire if I were dead or alive, did you? You've become that busy, ha?" You know, I don't really like to hurt anyone. Man's life is here this second, gone the next. Tell me, why should we hurt

121

anyone? That's why I say Yes to everything. Still, you know, Acharya-re: my wife is a nuisance. Every month she wants to visit her mother. I said Yes to her at first. Later I said No. I even beat her. But then I feel pity for her. You must have heard the village song:

> He beats his wife
>> But cries in his heart,
> so falls at her feet
>> and at her feet he pleads
> Who's sweeter, tell me,
>> Me or your Mother's place?

I'm like that. . . . We're here now.'

They had reached the tile-covered house beyond the grove. 'Is she in or not? She might've gone to the festival,' said Putta, and called out, 'Padmavati!' Praneshacharya who sat down on the pyol mat, heard a sweet female voice answer, 'Coming!' Warm attractive voice. Fear: who's she? Why did Putta bring me all the way here? The same voice said courteously: 'O you, you've come.' Praneshacharya started, turned around. She had crossed the threshold and stood there holding the pillar with one raised hand. As his eyes fell on her, she pulled her sari over her breast. Putta said, 'Look, who do you think I've brought here? An Acharya.' 'O you came this far,' she said again shyly. 'Shall I get some Ganges water?' she asked. 'You must take some milk and fruit at least,' she insisted, and went in. Praneshacharya was sweating all over. There was no doubt—she was a halfcaste Malera woman. Living alone. Why did Putta bring me here? Not a word from Putta. All his chatter had been stilled. The Acharya had suddenly the scary feeling that two eyes were getting at him from behind. For those onlooking eyes I'm a wide-open thing. Afraid to turn around, yet wanting to do so. Who knows what those eyes will say? As soon as eye meets eye, who knows what shape the unformed will take? Elongated dark eyes. A black snake braid coming down her shoulder, over her breast. The girl swaying at the end of the bamboo pole. Knives—wings—beaks—feathers. In the forest dark, the offering of full breasts. Belli's earth-coloured breasts. An unblinking eye that'll see everything as if it is wide-open. Behind him. The bird is paralysed by the stare of the black serpent. Dread. He turned around. It was true. The eyes were looking at him stealthily, her hands were holding a platter; the eyes peeping from the door suddenly retreated into the dark indoors. Bangles jingled. Again she came into the light. It was peaceful now. An expectation turned in his body, cutting a path inside. She bent forward to put down the platter, the top of her sari sliding, breasts thrust forward, eyes heavy with a look of pleading. A stirring of fire in his chest. His eyes looked on, fiery. The sense vanished of having become a wide-open object for staring eyes. Now he was those eyes. That art Thou. She asked, 'Where is the gentleman from?' Looking at the Acharya, his glowing person. Putta said, 'He's from Kundapura,' and added a lie, 'He knows Shinappa.' 'Looks after temple affairs,' adding another lie. When he said, 'He's come to this province to collect dues,' Putta gave him an entirely new personality. In the eyes of strangers, one gets a new form, a new make-up. 'Even to the point of doubting who I really am, I have become many persons in one single day. All right, let things happen as they will.' He sat waiting. 'Bird ravaging, bird ravaged, the knives. Wife Bhagirathi screamed as if the very quick of her life had been touched, before she fell back utterly motionless, dead. Then she burned in the cremation fire, Bhagirathi, the altar of my sacrifice. I lost her and entered limbo, a lost soul. Seen by these eyes. I have moved to the next stage of soul, leaving the ghostly stage behind. Perhaps.'

Padmavati, evading any possible direct gaze, went and sat at the foot of the door. Praneshacharya was disturbed again that she was staring at him from that vantage point. Plucking up courage he turned his head. His heart was pounding. Padmavati got up, and brought a platter of betelnut and betel leaf. Putta smeared lime on the betel leaves, folded and tucked several between his fingers, threw a piece of betelnut into his mouth and started speaking. Padmavati went back to sit at the foot of the door. Putta said:

'I met the Acharya on the road. We came chatting all the way. He'd started out for Kundapura. I said: why not stay here tonight and go to Tirthahalli tomorrow and catch a bus? Don't you agree that's a good idea?'

Padmavati too insisted, a little embarrassed:

'Right. Why not sleep here tonight and go tomorrow?'

Praneshacharya felt faint. His ears seemed to roar, his hands were clammy. 'No, no, not today. Tomorrow. I didn't reckon on the decisive moment being now, here. Not today, I'm in a period of mourning and pollution, I've just cremated my wife. Haven't yet disposed of Naranappa's body. I must tell them. I must speak the truth. I must get up and leave here. I must vanish.' But the body stayed there, solid, an object of Padmavati's expectant gaze. Putta said:

'All right then. He hasn't had his dinner yet. He'll go to the temple feast and come back here.' Then he asked Padmavati, familiarly, 'The Dharmasthala troupe has come here, hasn't it? Are you going to see their show?'

'O no. I'll just visit the temple in the evening, get God's *darshan* and come back here. I'll wait for you people.'

Without any move on his part, without so much as a grunt from him sitting between Putta and Padmavati, Putta said, 'Let's get up.' The Acharya stood up, looked at Padmavati. Long hair, not yet oiled after a bath; plump fleshy thighs, buttocks, breasts. Tall, long-limbed. A gleam in the eyes, an expectation. A waiting. Must have had a ritual bath in the river after her monthly period. Breasts rise and fall as she breathes in and out. They'll harden at the tips if caressed in the dark. The scent of grass and country sarsaparilla. Floating chariots of lightning-bugs. Fire. The crematory flames licking the firewood, reaching the hands and feet, simmering in the stomach and hissing, exploding, splitting the bony skull, stretching tongues of flame to the chest of the dead. The fire. Naranappa's dead body. Unburned yet. How he sat there once, on his front verandah pulling on his hubble-bubble. The body swung on the bamboo-stretcher, curving it with its weight. The Vedic sage Yajnavalkya said: 'Love. Love for whom? Love for one's wife is love for oneself. Love for God is love for oneself.' He'll search out the roots. He'll win. He looked on, he admired. Sage Vyasa was born in a pot, born complete with an ascetic's waterpot. The Acharya took a step. 'All right, then you go and come back. I'll wait for you,' said Padmavati. 'Lord Maruti really gave me the slip. Friend Mahabala played a trick on me. Naranappa took his revenge. The brahmins were greedy for the gold. Chandri waiting in the dark—took what she wanted—walked away. Bhagirathi shrieked and died.' Putta put his hand on his shoulder, stopped him at the edge of a wet field. Asked, 'What do you say?' Then he said, 'It turned out as I thought. Don't think that the woman's a common prostitute. No, sir. No lowcaste man has been near her. And she isn't the kind of spirit that'll accept any ordinary brahmin either. Not for money, not for a few coins. Didn't you see for yourself? She has an estate. Even the ancient sages would fall for her, she's like that. I was scared for a minute you might expose my lie. You liked her, didn't you? This Putta will do anything for a friend. Putta, the Altruist, that's my title,' he said, laughing, patting the Acharya's back.

Crossing the wet field, the fences, walking over the makeshift bridge, through the lane, again into the bustle of the crowded fair. A crowd milled around the temple chariot. Another crowd around the sodawater shop. Still another, around the man with the performing monkey. Children's toy trumpets, balloons. In the midst of these noises, a demon, an evil spirit. A town-crier. Beating his tom-tom, he announced in his loud town-crier voice: 'There's a plague in Shivamogge! The epidemic of Mari! Anyone going to Shivamogge should stop at Tirthahalli and get an inoculation! That's the order of the Municipality!' People listened to him with interest, and drank more sodawater. Laughed in guffaws at the antics of the monkey. A bilingual expert spoke in Urdu and Kannada, selling his medicine to the gathered crowd: 'Just one anna, one anna, *ek ana, ek ana*. For stomach-aches, ear-aches, diabetes, arthritis, children's diseases, menstrual troubles, itches and typhoid—take this pill. Pundits from Kerala have prepared this pill with magic chants. Just one anna, *ek ana, ek ana* . . .' The Bombay Box man was dancing: 'Look, look at the Tirupati God, Timmappa! Look, look at the courtesan of Bombay!' An acrobat slid in a flash down the slope of a rope tied between a branch above and a peg on the floor, and came to his feet with a salute. A man suddenly slapped a little boy for wanting a balloon. The boy cried loudly. A gramophone song from the coffee shop. Sweetmeats of many colours in the Muslim shop. The drawling intonation of the peasants and their women. An incessant priestly jumble of Sanskrit scripture on the temple chariot, the raucous talk of the Smarta brahmins. In between he must decide, here, now. Decide to give up a quarter-century of discipline and become a man of the world? No, no. Naranappa's funeral comes before all else. After that come all other decisions. Garuda and Lakshmana would have returned today after consulting the Guru. What should he say if the Guru said No? The same dilemma, all over again.

He stood near the temple. A blind beggar was singing to the tune of a drone-box. A devotional song. 'O how shall I please you, how shall I serve you, O Lord?' When Putta threw a coin into his platter, another beggar with only stumps for hands and legs came crawling towards him, flailing his stumps, crying 'No hands, no legs for this sinner!' He whined and pleaded, lay flat on the floor, lifted his dwarfed arms and legs, and beat himself. displaying the places where the fingers had been eaten away and become stubs. Seeing this body decomposing in leprosy, Praneshacharya thought again of Naranappa's body rotting, uncremated. Putta threw a coin for the beggar. More deformed bodies rushed towards him, crawling, beating their stomachs, beating their mouths. 'Let's go, let's go,' said the Acharya.

Putta said, 'You go in and eat your temple dinner.'

'Why don't you come along?' invited Praneshacharya. All of a sudden, he'd felt panic at the thought of being seen, alone, unaccompanied, by the rows of brahmins sitting down for the feast in the temple hall. 'I can't stir without Putta,' he thought. He'd never before felt such a dread of being alone.

'What are you talking about? Did you forget I'm no brahmin, but a Malera?' said Putta, to which the Acharya said,

'Never mind, come along.'

'What, are you joking? This place is full of people who know me. If not, I'd have tried it. You know, don't you, of the time a goldsmith boy told lies and got a job in the monastery? But then, we Maleras too have our sacred threads, don't we? I'm just talking for talking's sake. I really don't have the gall, the guts to sit and eat a meal with you. You'd better go, I'll wait here.'

Praneshacharya, not able to stand the pathetic cries of the invading beggars all around him, walked into the temple in a daze.

On all the four raised verandahs of the temple, they had

set rows of banana leaves. Before each leaf sat a food-seeking brahmin. As he saw their faces, Praneshacharya's heart sank. What would happen if they spot me? Let me run. But he couldn't lift his feet. He stood there rooted, and thought: 'What am I doing? What lowborn misdeed am I committing? I'm in the unclean period of mourning and can I in full knowledge sit with the brahmins and eat a meal? And pollute them all with my impurity? These people believe that the temple chariot will not move an inch if there's any pollution around. If I seat myself here and eat with them, it's as heinous a sin as Naranappa catching temple-fish to destroy brahmin ways. If they discover, in the middle of the meal, that this is Praneshacharya . . . that he's still in the pollution period after his wife's death . . . it'll be a scandal. The entire chariot-festival will get cancelled. Thousands of eyes will devour him.'

'Here, here's a free leaf, come here,' said somebody. He was startled. He looked. A brahmin sitting at one end of the row was inviting him. What should he do? O Lord, what should he do? He just stood there. 'Didn't you hear me?' said the inviting brahmin, laughing, reaching out for Praneshacharya's hand, and pointing to the free place and the leaf. 'Look there. I reserved that leaf for you, and left a cup on it for you. If I had not, you'd have had to wait for the next meal-line,' he said. The Acharya mechanically walked to it and sat down. He felt dizzy in the head.

Trying to calm down his mind, he thought, 'O God, what's the root of this dread? Are these the first pains of a rebirth? Is it the kind of fear that will be quenched if I sleep with Padmavati tonight? Will it be quenched if I go live with Chandri? What's my decision worth? Am I forever to be a ghost of a man, hovering in indecision? I wish Putta was here. Shall I get up, walk out? What will the brahmin next to me think?'

A brahmin walked through the row of seated diners, touching each leaf-end with holy water. Another poured a spoonful of milk-porridge on the edge of each leaf. From behind him, two robust brahmins came serving rice, crying out, 'Clear the way, the way, the way.' Then there was a salad of lentils and cucumbers. There were new fears at the appearance of each face, as they came close to serve the food: 'Maybe this one knows me and will recognize me, what will I do?'

The brahmin who sat next to him, who gave him the place, was a huge dark figure like Bhimasena. A Smarta, with sandalpaste marks drawn lengthwise on his forehead. The Acharya feared him as soon as he set eyes on him. Furthermore, he had questions that made the Acharya nervous.

'Can I ask from where you come?'

'I'm right from this place.'

'From where exactly? From down the mountain?'

'Kundapura.'

'What community, if I may ask?'

'Vaishnava.'

'What sub-group?'

'Shivalli.'

'I'm of the Kota group. What's your descent-line?'

'Bharadvaja.'

'I'm of the Angirasa line. O sir, I'm really glad I met you. We've a young girl, getting ready for marriage. In a year or two, she'll reach puberty. We can't let our girls reach puberty, before we find them husbands; we're not yet that spoiled. So we're really looking now for a suitable bridegroom. Sir, do let me know if there's any suitable groom in your group. Relieving a father's burden is a great help. After we finish this meal, let's go to our house. I'll give you a copy of the girl's horoscope. You can stay with us tonight.'

Praneshacharya, getting his *saru* served into a leaf-cup,

lifted his head and looked up. The man serving it was intently looking at him. He stood still for a second, then moved on.

'All right,' said Praneshacharya, trying to cut the conversation short. Is it possible that this man serving *saru* knows his face? He has a charcoal caste-mark on his forehead, obviously a Madhva, like himself—it's quite likely the man would know the Acharya. He can't even get up now, after taking the holy water in his palm, after imbibing it in the name of the Lord, chanting with all the others: 'Shrimad Ramaramana Govinda . . aa . . Govinda.' He mixed the *saru* with the hot steaming rice and ate it. It was some days since he'd had a regular meal. 'O Lord, tide me over this calamity. See to it that I am not detected today. I cannot decide and say, "This is my own decision." I seem to involve everyone else in what I do. After what happened, I should have performed the rites for Naranappa myself. But how could I do it alone? The ritual needs three more, even to carry the body out. I have to ask three others. Which means, I involve three others in my decision. This is the root of my agony, my anxiety. Even when I slept with Chandri, unknown to everyone, I involved the life of the entire agrahara in my act. As a result, my life is open to the world.' The man serving *saru* came again, shouting, '*Saru, saru,* who wants *saru*?' He stood before the Acharya's leaf and said, '*Saru.*' The Acharya looked up, timidly.

The man said, 'I think I've seen you somewhere.'

'Quite possible,' said the Acharya. But by God's grace the man went to the next row, to attend to their leaves. 'But his eyes are thinking of me. They're sending my image to his brain and trying to check out my identity. Even if I went with Chandri, someone will waylay me and ask, "Who are you? Which sub-caste? Which descent? Which group?" Unless I shed brahminhood altogether I cannot stand aside, liberated from all this. If I shed it, I'll fall into the tigerish world of cock-fights, I'll burn like a worm. How shall I escape this state of neither-here-nor-there, this ghostliness?'

The brahmin next to him grumbled, 'They've watered down the *saru* this time. . . . What, you are filling your belly with mere *saru*. Do wait, sweets and things are yet to come.'

The fellow who had brought the *saru*, came back this time with a vessel full of vegetable curry. He stopped in front of the Acharya and said, 'I can't remember where. Could it be in the monastery? On worship days I often go there for cooking jobs. Our agrahara is beyond the river. I did go to the monastery the day before yesterday to do some cooking, then I came here.'

Then, in a hurry, he walked off to serve the next row, announcing, 'Curry, curry, curry.'

The Acharya thought he should get up now and walk out. but his legs had gone numb. The brahmin next to him said, 'You know, our girl is a very good cook. Very obedient to elders. We want very much to give her to a respectable family where the father- and mother-in-law are still alive to guide family affairs.'

'There's only one way out of the present fear. I must take on the responsibility of Naranappa's last rites. I must stand upright in the eyes of the brahmins, in the very agrahara where I grew up to be respected, an elder. Must call in Garuda and Lakshmana and tell them: "This is how it went. My decision is such and such. I'll shed the respectability I acquired here before your eyes. I've come back to tear it and throw it down, right here before your eyes." If I don't, my fear will dog me everywhere, I won't be free. What then?

'Just like Naranappa who turned the agrahara upside down by fishing in the temple-tank, I too would have turned the brahmin lives upside down. I'd be giving their faith a shattering blow. What shall I tell them? "I slept with Chandri. I felt disgust for my wife. I drank coffee in a com-

131

mon shop in a fair. I went to see a cock-fight. I lusted after Padmavati. Even at a time of mourning and pollution, I sat in a temple-line with brahmins and ate a holy feast. I even invited a Malera boy to come into the temple and join me. This is my truth. Not a confession of wrongs done. Not a repentance for sins commited. Just plain truth. My truth. The truth of my inner life. Therefore this is my decision. Through my decision, here! I cut myself off."'

'If necessary, we won't object to giving her a dowry, sir. You know, the times are wicked; dark-skinned girls have a hard time getting husbands. You come and see the girl yourself. The only defect is her dark complexion, but her eyes and nose are very shapely. According to her horoscope, she has a rare Lion-Elephant combination for a good future. She'll be the very Goddess of Good Luck to any house she sets foot in,' said the brahmin next to him, eating his curry and rice.

'But if I don't tell the agrahara brahmins, if Naranappa's body is not properly cremated, I cannot escape fear. If I decide to live with Chandri without telling anyone, the decision is not complete, not fearless. I must come now to a final decision. All things indirect must become direct. Must pierce straight in the eye. But it's agony either way. If I hide things, all through life I'll be agonized by the fear of discovery, by some onlooking eye. If I don't, I'll muddy the lives of others by opening up and exposing the truth to the very eyes my brahminhood has lived and grown by. Have I the authority to include another's life in my decision? The pain of it, the cowardice of it. O God, take from me the burden of decision. Just as it happened in the dark of the jungle, without my will, may this decision too happen. May it happen all at once. May a new life come into being before I blink my eye. Naranappa, did you go through this agony? Mahabala, did you go through it?'

The man who had brought *saru* came this time with a

basket of sweets. The brahmin next to the Acharya didn't want the sweets served on his leaf, but received them in his left hand and put them aside. The man was again standing in front of his leaf. The Acharya's heart heaved.

'O yes, my memory be damned. You are Praneshacharya from Durvasapura, aren't you? O how can someone like you come for a humble meal here? There was a big feast in the Sahukar's house. For all the big people like you, they arranged the feast there. Because you didn't have any mark on your forehead, I didn't recognize you right away. Neither did you tell me. If I don't tell the Sahukar, I'll really get it in the neck—that I seated and fed a great Pundit at the end of a meal-line. I'll be back in a minute. Wait. Please.' Saying which he ran, leaving the basket of sweets behind. Praneshacharya quickly took a palmful of ritual water, drank it up, ending his meal thereby. He leapt to his feet and walked away. 'Swami, Swami, the milk-porridge is yet to come,' screamed the brahmin of the next leaf. But he didn't turn back till he came out of the temple. He had come out, his hands yet unwashed—away from people, far away. Before he had gone far, he heard a voice: 'Acharya-re . . . Acharya-re!' Putta's voice. He came running and stood close to Praneshacharya, who quickened his pace.

'What's this, Swami? Not a word, and you're running like someone in a hurry to go to the bathroom for a big job,' laughed Putta. When he was far from the crowd, the Acharya stopped. He looked at his unwashed hands and was disgusted.

'What, the call was so urgent you couldn't even wait to wash your hands! It's happened to me too. Come let's go to the tank, you can do it there.'

They walked to the tank. Putta said, on the way:

'I decided one thing, Acharya-re. I'll come with you to Kundapura. I didn't tell you earlier, my wife and children went to their mother's place over a month ago. Haven't had

a letter from them. I've to talk to her and bring her back.
You're an elder. You must do me a favour. Come and give
my wife some good advice. She'll listen to you. You became
my life's companion in a single day. One more thing,
Acharya-re. I don't carry tales. I won't breathe a word about
your sleeping in Padmavati's house—I'll take an oath on my
mother's body, I won't tattle. There I was standing, watching
the monkey's dance. Then I saw you running, it made me
laugh. These things do happen. Calls of nature become most
urgent right in the middle of dinner. I thought that's what
happened to you, so I felt like laughing.'

Praneshacharya climbed down into the tank, and washed
his hands. Above him, Putta stood, his back against the tank
bricks. When Praneshacharya came back and stood next to
him, he said,

'What? Back so soon?'

'One thing, Putta.'

Praneshacharya looked up. The long evening of a summer
day. Streaks of red on the west. Line after line of white birds
returning to their nests. Down below, at the edge of the tank,
a stork is gurgling. It's almost time for lighting the lamps.
How many days ago was it that the lamps were lit in the
agrahara, that the returning evening cows and calves were
tied up and milked, and the milk offered to the Lord? The
clear faraway forms of the western hills grow dim, like a
world melting in a dream. The colours of this moment fading
the next, the sky grows bare. As the new-moon day is left
behind, in a little while a sliver of the moon will appear over
the hills, like the edge of a silver chalice bent over an idol for
an inaugural libation. Silence will fill the valleys between the
hills. The torches lit for the night service will die down as the
service gets over, and the noises of the fair will fade. Again,
the drama troupe's drums will raise and spread their din. 'If I
begin walking now, I'll reach the agrahara by midnight, far

away from this world. In full view of the frightened brahmins, I'll stand exposed like the naked quick of life; and I, elder in their midst, will turn into a new man at midnight. Maybe when the fire leaps and dances around Naranappa's dead body, there'll be a certain consolation. When I tell them about myself, there should be no taint of repentance in me, no trace of any sorrow that I am a sinner. If not, I cannot go beyond conflict and dualities. I must see Mahabala. Must tell him: only the form we forge for ourselves in our inmost will is ours without question. If that's true, don't you really have any craving for good any more?—I must ask him.' That melodious Sanskrit line came into his mind again: 'Southern breezes from sandalwood mountains caress delicate vines of clove'. Praneshacharya was quite moved. Affection moved him. He put a hand over Putta's shoulders, and drew him closer. And patting his back for the first time, he said, 'What was I about to say?'

'O sir, when I met you on the road, your talk was so stiff that I thought this gentleman will never be friends with me,' said Putta, delighted that the Acharya put a friendly hand on his shoulder.

'Look here, Putta. Do you know why I left that dinner in a hurry? I've to get back to Durvasapura at once.'

'Oho, how can you do that, Acharya-re? Your Padmavati will be waiting there for you, with a soft bed all ready; joss-sticks all lit up, and flowers in her hair. If you aren't there with me, how can I face her? Whatever your urgent business, you must stay here tonight and go only by morning. A curse on my head if you leave now,' said Putta, and tugged at Praneshacharya. Praneshacharya got a little frightened. He doubted the firmness of his own will. He might slide back. He must now escape Putta.

'No, Putta. Impossible. Shall I tell you the truth? I didn't want to involve your feelings, so I didn't tell you so far.' He thought for a moment, and decided it was best to tell a lie. 'My brother is deathly sick in Durvasapura. I heard the news while I was sitting there in the temple. It may be any minute now, how can I . . . ?'

Putta sighed. Disappointed, he agreed, 'All right then.'

Praneshacharya, preparing to go, said, 'When do I see you again? Tell Padmavati I'll see her on my way back to Kundapura. Shall I move on then?'

Putta stood there, thinking. 'How can I send you alone through the dark forest? I'll come with you,' he said.

Praneshacharya was nonplussed. It seemed impossible to chase away this man by any tactic. 'I don't really want you to be bothered on my account,' he said. Putta didn't budge.

'No bother, no trouble. I too have some business in Durvasapura. I've cousins in Parijatapura. You probably know my friend Naranappa there. When I went to Parijatapura once, I got to know him just as I got to know you now. O yes! I'm glad I remembered. The whole town knows Naranappa squandered his property. He can't pass up anything wrapped in a sari, he's that type. This is strictly between ourselves, Acharya-re. If you happen to know him, please don't mention anything about Padmavati, and the way she invited you. Okay, why hide it from you? As soon as I got acquainted with Naranappa, he stuck to me like a leech, insisting I introduce him to Padmavati. But I don't do such things, I'm not that cheap. Still, you know, what can you do when a brahmin falls all over you? Padmavati didn't like his ways. He was such a horrible drunkard, she told me later. "Don't you bring him here any more," she said. You'd better keep all this to yourself. I started on something and ended somewhere else. I told you, didn't I, my village is a little beyond Tirthahalli. Naranappa owns an orchard there. It's now razed to the ground, ruined out of sheer neglect. It's years since he received from it a single arecanut due to him. Knowing him as I do, will he say No to me if I ask? So I'd like to try and ask him: "Rent out the orchard to me. I'll work on it, improve it, it'll also bring you some profit." That's why I said, I'll come with you, Acharya-re. You too will have company on the dark road. And I'll get some work done.'

Praneshacharya listened to Putta restlessly. 'Shall I tell him Naranappa is dead? Shall I tell him my true dilemma?' But he didn't want to raise a big storm in that simple heart. In case he really decides to come along, it would be impossible not to tell him. Then it suddenly seemed a good thing to have Putta for company. 'How can I face all those brahmins alone? First, let me try it all on Putta, bosom-friend of the present. Let's see how I look in his eyes—that may be a good way of doing it.' Now the sky had become cloudless, bare. From the temple issued noises of gongs beaten, conches blown for worship. Must go now. 'Let's go then,' he said.

Just then a covered wagon came trundling along. Putta said, 'Wait a minute.' He held out his hand and stopped the cart. From within the cart, a Smarta man in a gold-lace shawl put out his head and asked, 'What do you want?'

'Does your cart, by any chance, go via Agumbe?' said Putta.

'Ha,' nodded the lace-shawled gentleman from within the cart.

'Do you have place for two? We want to get to Durvasa-pura,' said Putta.

'But we've place only for one.'

Putta took hold of his hand and said, 'You'd better go, Acharya-re.'

'No, no, Let's go together, on foot,' said the Acharya.

'*Che, Che*, you shouldn't walk all the way and tire yourself out. I'll come and see you tomorrow,' said Putta. The man in the shawl wanted them to hurry. 'Then, are you coming? We'll turn off a mile or two before we reach Durvasapura.

One of you can come with us. Get into the cart. Quick.'

Putta insisted on Praneshacharya getting in, and pushed him in. Praneshacharya, not seeing any way out, climbed into the cart and sat down. The cart started moving. 'I'll see you tomorrow,' said Putta. 'All right,' said Praneshacharya. Four or five more hours of travel. Then, what?

The sky was full of stars. The moon, a sliver. A perfectly clear constellation of the Seven Sages. A sudden noise of drum beats. Here and there, the flames of a torch. The hard breathing of the bullocks climbing the hillock. The sound of the cow-bells round their necks. He will travel, for another four or five hours. Then, after that, what?

Praneshacharya waited, anxious, expectant.

AFTERWORD

The title, *Samskara*, refers to a concept central to Hinduism. Our epigraph lists some of the denotations.

'A rite of passage or life-cycle ceremony', 'forming well, making perfect', 'the realizing of past perceptions', 'preparation, making ready', are some of the meanings of the multivocal Sanskrit word. Even 'Sanskrit' (*samskṛta*, the 'remade, refined, perfected' language) is part of the *samskara*-paradigm. The sub-title for this translation, 'A Rite for a Dead Man', is the most concrete of these many concentric senses that spread through the work.

The opening event is a death, an anti-brahminical brahmin's death—and it brings in its wake a plague, many deaths, questions without answers, old answers that do not fit the new questions, and the rebirth of one good brahmin, Praneshacharya. In trying to resolve the dilemma of who, if any, should perform the heretic's death-rite (a *samskara*), the Acharya begins a *samskara* (a transformation) for himself. A rite for a dead man becomes a rite of passage for the living.

In life as in death, Naranappa questioned the brahmins of the village, exposed their *samskara* (refinement of spirit, maturation through many lives) or lack of it. He lived the life of a libertine in the heart of an exclusive orthodox colony (*agrahara*), broke every known taboo; drank liquor, ate flesh, caught fish with his Muslim friends in the holy temple-tank, and lived with a lowcaste woman. He had cast off his lawfully-wedded brahmin wife, and antagonized his kin. Protected fully by modern secular laws, and even more fully by the brahmins' own bad conscience, he lived defiantly in their midst. If they could exorcize him, they would have found in him a fitting scapegoat to carry their own inmost unspoken libidinous desires. He was their mocking anti-self and he knew it. Now that he is dead, they could punish him at least in death, by disowning him.

Was he brahmin enough in life to be treated as one in death? Did he have the necessary 'preparation' (*samskara*) to deserve a proper 'ceremony' (*samskara*)? Once a brahmin, always a brahmin? Age-old questions, human questions in Hindu form, they are treacherous and double-edged: once raised, they turn on the questioner.

Naranappa's targets are the strait-laced village brahmins who attend to the 'rituals' (*samskaras*), but have not earned by any means their 'refinement of spirit' (*samskara*). They are greedy, gluttonous, mean-spirited; they love gold, betray orphans and widows; they are jealous of Naranappa's every forbidden pleasure. They turn for answers to Praneshacharya, Naranappa's opposite number. But, ironically, in the very act of seeking the answer in the Books, and later in seeking a sign from Maruti the chaste Monkey-god, the Acharya abandons everything and becomes one with his opposite: contrary to all his 'preparation' he sleeps with Chandri, Naranappa's lowcaste mistress. By what authority now can he judge Naranappa or advise his brahmin followers? So far his *samskara* consisted of Sanskrit learning and ascetic practice. He had turned even marriage into a penance, immolated himself by marrying an invalid. His sudden sexual experience with the forbidden Chandri becomes an unorthodox 'rite of initiation'. So the question, 'Who is a brahmin, how is he made?' finally turns even against this irreproachable brahmin of brahmins, brahmin by birth as by *samskara* (in its many senses). Through crisis, through a breach in the old 'formations', he begins to transform himself. With the rightness of paradox, he is initiated through an illicit deed, a misdeed, totally counter to his past. He participates in the

140

condition of his opposite, Naranappa, through Naranappa's own hand-picked whore.

All the battles of tradition and defiance, asceticism and sensuality, the meaning and meaninglessness of ritual, dharma as nature and law, desire (*kama*) and salvation (*moksha*), have now become internal to Praneshacharya. The arena shifts from a Hindu village community to the body and spirit of the protagonist.

Though the word *samskara* does not occur obtrusively or too frequently in the narrative, its meanings implicitly inform the action. Furthermore, the action depends on the several meanings being at loggerheads with each other. It is significant that, in the brahminical texts, there is no division between 'outer' and 'inner', 'social' and 'individual', 'ritual' and 'spiritual' aspects: they imply and follow each other in one seamless unity. 'Just as a work of painting gradually unfolds itself on account of the several colours (with which it is drawn), so *brahmanya* (brahminhood) is similarly brought out by *samskaras* performed according to prescribed rites.'

As in many traditional tales a question is raised; kept alive, despite possible solutions; maintained, till profounder questions are raised. Answers are delayed until the question is no longer relevant. The delay is filled with 'promised answers, suspended, jammed or partial answers, snares and ambiguities'. The 'perpetually deferred reply' plots the story. Question, Delay and Answer (or its absence) form the overt strategy for another exploration, for covering (and uncovering) psychological ground. Meanwhile, the physical problem of the body's disposal has, ironically, ceased to be relevant; the body is simply, unceremoniously carried in a cart and burned in a field by Chandri and her Muslim friends, though the Acharya does not know it.

In Praneshacharya, brahminism questions itself in a modern existentialist mode (a mode rather alien to it, in

141

fact); and the questioning leads him into new and ordinary worlds. These include not only Naranappa's world but also Putta's. Naranappa has an ideology; Putta has none. In the guided tour through temple-festival and fair, whorehouse and pawnshop, the Acharya sees a demoniac world of passion and sensation, where the human watchers of cock-fights are one with the fighting roosters. Putta is a denizen of this world; he is riddle-master, expert bargainer, pimp without any *samskara*; he is so completely and thoughtlessly at one with this world that he is a marvel. He is Praneshacharya's initiator into the mysteries of the ordinary and the familiar, the purity of the unregenerate, the wholeness of the crude. The vision of this world is part of the Acharya's new *samskara*, his 'passage'.

Indeed, the story moves very much like a *rite de passage*. It is well known that many types of ritual, especially rites of initiation, have three stages: 'separation', 'transition' ('margin or limen') and 're-incorporation'. In and through such rituals, individuals and groups change their state or status. Such a change of state is often symbolized (as in this book) by a change of place—a going-away, a seclusion and a coming back.

Particularly rich in symbols of 'tradition' is the Acharya's flight from his accustomed village: he wanders through forests and lonely roads, meets with the riddling Putta, journeys through a non-verbal world of fairs, festivals, and performances where he is the marginal man, liminal like the unhoused dead, 'betwixt and between'. Again, he experiences in himself the condition of Naranappa, once his opposite.

So a *samskara* is not only the subject of the work but the form as well. The Acharya moves through the three stages— though we see him not entirely into the third stage, but only on its threshold.

Will he, can he, ever integrate it with his old ways, his past *samskara*? We do not know. We only see him mutating, changing from a fully evolved socialized brahmin at one with his tradition towards a new kind of person; choosing himself, individuating himself, and 'alienating' himself. We are left 'anxious, expectant', like the Acharya himself at the end of the novel. Thus, a traditional pattern, like Question, Delay and Answer, or a three-part ritual, appears here without the usual climax or closure. Such inconclusive, anti-climactic use of tradition is very much a part of this modern tale.

I think I have said enough, perhaps too much, about the resonances of the title. *Samskara* is a religious novel, a contemporary re-working of ancient themes. So, naturally (according to some, too easily), the work tends to allegory, and finds continuous use for mythology. The characters are somewhat simplified, and represent polar opposites. The characters come in sets: e.g. Praneshacharya v. Mahabala-Naranappa-Shripati; their lowcaste mistresses v. the brahmin women. Neatly, schematically, the opposites are mediated. Praneshacharya merges with his opposite number through Chandri, the latter's lover; the Acharya's erotic description of a classical heroine rouses Shripati, and he makes love to an outcaste woman on the riverbank.

The complex relations between asceticism and eroticism are well-worked in Hindu thought and mythology. The mythology of Shiva details the paradoxes of the erotic ascetic, the god-heretic. The erotic plagues and tempts the ascetic; the two are also seen as alternative modes of quest, represented here by Naranappa and the Acharya. They speak the same language.

Naranappa's mischief revels in mythological reminders and precedents. Didn't Parashara the great ascetic put a cloud on the holy Ganges as the fisherwoman ferried him across, take her in the boat, bless her body with perpetual fragrance? Out of this union of sage and fishwife came Vyasa the seer, compiler of the Vedas and epic poet of the *Mahabharata*. Didn't Vishvamitra the warrior-sage succumb to the celestial Menaka and lose all his accumulated powers? He once ate even dog-meat to survive a famine and became the proverbial example of 'emergency ethics' (*apaddharma*). And didn't Shankara, the celibate philosopher, use his yogic powers to enter a dead king's body, to experience sex, to qualify for a debate on the subject with a woman?

Praneshacharya often wonders whether there is not a serious side to Naranappa's mockery and sensuality; whether sacrilege is not a 'left-handed' way of attaining the sacred. By an ancient inversion, salvation is as possible through intoxication as by self-discipline, through violation as through observance of the Law. The Lord may even be reached sooner through hate than by devotion. Naranappa's way gathers strength by enlisting, not defying, instinctual urges. Praneshacharya himself remembers out of his past in Benares, another Naranappa-like figure, fellow-pupil Mahabala. Mahabala gave up the 'strait and narrow' path of Sanskrit learning and found 'reality' in a whore in the holy city itself.

The other polarity is quite blatant: while all the brahmin wives are sexless, unappetizing, smelly, invalids at best, the women of other castes are seen as glowing sex-objects and temptations to the brahmin. Lowcaste and outcaste women like Chandri and Belli are hallowed and romanticized by references to classical heriones like Shakuntala, and Menaka, the temptress of sages. Besides being classical, women like Chandri are also earthly and amoral, ideals of untroubled sexuality.

As in an early Bergman film, the characters are frankly allegorical, but the setting is realistic. An abstract human theme is reincarnated in just enough particulars of a space, a time, a society. Though the name of the village is allegoric, named after Durvasa the angry sage—all the nearby villages and cities are real places on the map, Shivamogge, Basrur, etc. Several details suggest that the time of action could be the early '30s or '40s: references to older coins (*anna*), and to the then-popular daily *Tayinadu*, the rise of the Congress Party, etc. Yet the time is a stereotype of what might be called Indian Village Time—indefinite, continuous, anywhere between a few decades ago and the medieval centuries. The cycles of natural season and the calendar of human ceremony are interlocked in Village Time. The rigid greedy brahmins mindlessly live off it, while Praneshacharya mindfully lives in it until it is interrupted and cancelled; then he drifts out of the accustomed village spaces and cycles into the outer world and comes back. The dead man, the heretic, defied it all and lived in his own time and territory, his body.

'Realism' and 'allegory' (I hope the terms are clear in context) are generic patterns of expectations; the attempted realism of place, time and custom raises certain expectations in the reader. Occasionally, this felt mixture of modes makes uneasy reading. 'Realistically' speaking, there are many things wrong with the story. I have heard it said that the central dilemma regarding the death-rite need be no dilemma to a learned brahmin like the Acharya, 'Crest-Jewel of Vedic Learning'; there is an answer to this very question in a text, the *Dharmasindhu*. Certain simple ritual modifications and offerings would have solved the problem, as the guru of Dharmasthala clearly suggests. And every villager is supposed to know that no crow or vulture would touch a plague-ridden rat. Several dramatic pages on the plague flout such native knowledge.

But the book's allegoric and narrative power marshals enough poetic images, ideas, stereotypes, and caricatures around the central *human* figure of the Acharya and his mutation, so that most readers are 'bounced' into the novel and ask no questions. Indeed, in the Acharya, we see 'allegory' wrestling with 'realism'; in him an archetype wrestles with himself, and becomes atypical.

Not every reader is so taken. Certain brahmin communities in South India were offended by the picture of decadent brahminism. They felt that brahmin men and women were unfairly caricatured; they were offended by the novelist's rather intrusive partiality for Naranappa and the sudra women.

A more serious objection is that the central figure projects a narrow part of the Hindu ideal—not the integrity of the four stages of life, in which desire (*kama*) and the goods of this world (*artha*) are affirmed and celebrated in their time and place and it is part of the design of dharma to do so. To this way of thinking, the Acharya's brand of self-denial is aberrant. As his invalid wife Bhagirathi reminds him in the opening pages, he is in the second stage of life, a married house-holder. Yet he lives as one arrested in the first stage (celibate student), or as having progressed to the third (forest-dweller), or even the fourth (ascetic renouncer). As an Acharya he ought to have known better than to marry an invalid, a barren woman who would only cripple him in all the pursuits necessary for an able-bodied, able-spirited brahmin. Neither the author, nor his one rather idealized brahmin, seems to be aware of such discrepancies.

Yet it is such a discrepancy that makes the entire action possible. Despite all his virtue, the Acharya does not have the virtue of living out fully his present *stage*. Having exiled *kama* from his house and family, he had to find it outside his customary space, in the forest; his sense of dharma had to be undone and remade by it.

One could reasonably take the view that this novel, written

146

in the sixties, is really presenting a decadent Hinduism through the career of a limited hero, capable only of arcs, not full circles. As said earlier, the last phase of the Acharya's initiation is an anxious return, a waiting on the threshold; his questions seem to find no restful answers. What is suggested is a movement, not a closure. The novel ends, but does not conclude.

NOTES

These rather minimal notes are part of the translator's effort to 'translate' and a confession of failures. They include:

(a) glosses on myth, ritual, flora, food, names, quotations (exx. Madhva, Matsyagandhi, *saru*);

(b) the original Kannada or Sanskrit words (exx. *tamas, ekadashi,*) which I have replaced in the text by English glosses (exx. 'Darkness', 'eleventh day of the moon').

(a) is meant for the unspecialized non-Indian or non-Kannada reader, (b) for fellow-Indians and Indianists.

No transliterations, only approximate Roman spellings, have been used.

Page 1

Maruti: name of Hanuman, Monkey-god, and devotee of Rama (an incarnation of Vishnu). Hanuman is worshipped by devotees of Vishnu; his temple is usually outside the village, as here.

agrahara: 'villages or land assigned to Brahmins for their maintenance' (Kittel); an exclusive settlement of brahmins.

Praneshacharya: the title *acharya* 'spiritual guide, learned man' is added to certain brahmin names, especially among the Madhva sect (cf. notes on p. 5) to which most of the brahmins in this book belong.

Kashi or Benares: a holy city of North India, especially known for Sanskrit scholarship.

Page 2

five-fold nectar: *Panchamrita*, the five nectarious substances: milk, curd, ghee, honey, and sugar, and a compound made of them, offered to gods and distributed to devotees on special days.

Narayana: one of the many names of the god Vishnu, uttered frequently as exclamation, blessing, etc. Such names have the power to redeem and protect.

Page 3

saru: a well-seasoned sauce regularly eaten with rice.

consecrated water: *aposhana*, a ritual sipping of water from the palm of the hand at the beginning and end of a meal.

Page 4
   holy legend: *Purana*, a tale of the past, about gods, saints, etc.

Page 5
   lowcaste: *shudra*, the fourth caste.
   Madhvas and *Smartas*: brahmin sects, traditional rivals. Madhvas
are the followers of the philosopher Madhva (13th century) who taught
dvaita or dualism (soul and godhead are two entities, not one). Smartas
follow Shankara (7th century) who taught *advaita* or monism (soul and
godhead are one and the same). Madhvas are strict worshippers of
Vishnu, and bear only Vaishnava names. For instance, Durgabhatta (a
Smarta) is named after Durga the goddess, a manifestation of Shiva's
consort; nor does his name carry the suffix *acharya*. Note also how the
name of heretic Naranappa (set against the entire brahmin community)
is a form of Narayana (or Vishnu), localized to Naranappa, with none
of the Sanskritic 'markers' of orthodoxy like *acharya, bhatta*.

Page 6
   dharma: a central word in Hinduism, therefore multi-vocal, un-
translatable; usually glossed 'law, righteousness, duty, code, etc.'
   Shankara: philosopher of monism: according to legend, the celibate
philosopher was challenged in argument by a woman-philosopher and
disqualified because he had experienced no sex. He qualified himself,
without losing his celibate status, by magically entering the body of a
king just dead and having intercourse with the queen—and returned to
finish the argument.

Page 7
   wedding-string: *tali*, ceremonially tied by the bridegroom around the
bride's neck, as part of the wedding-ritual.
   holy stone: *saligrama*, a black river-stone, worshipped as sacred to
Vishnu.

Page 8
   '*sharp*': *cittini*, 'intelligent woman', one of the eight types of women
in Vatsyayana's *Kamasutra* (manual of love).

Page 11
   eleventh day of the moon: *ekadasi*, a day of fasting for orthodox
brahmins.

Page 13
   uppittu: salted (and spiced) dish made out of cream of wheat, rice,
flattened rice, etc.

widows: some brahmin orthodox sects like the Smarta (Durgabhatta's sect) insist on certain austerities for their widows; one of them is a shaven head.

Page 14

Manu: 'a generic name for fourteen successive mythical progenitors and sovereigns of the earth'; the first of these is supposed to be the author of the Code of Manu, the most influential codification of Hindu laws and rules of conduct.

parijata: the coral tree, one of the five trees in heaven. Note that all these flowers are sacred to Vishnu, as Durgabhatta's are sacred to Shiva.

Page 15

Konkani: a person from Konkan on the west coast.

hot months: *Chaitra* (March–April), the first month of the Hindu year, a month of Spring and *Vaishakha* (April–May), the second month.

Page 16

eighth month: *Kartika* (October–November).

rainy month: *Shravana* (July–August), the fifth lunar month.

Great Commentator: *Tikacharya*, a revered commentator on Madhva's (cf. note 2, p. 5) works.

Durvasa: a sage notorious for his chronic bad temper. The five Pandava brothers are the exiled heroes of the epic *Mahabharata*. Draupadi is their wife. Dharmaraja is the eldest, known for his patience and fairness; Bhima, the second brother, is known for his rashness and strength.

Page 17

twelfth day of the moon: *dvadasi*, on this day orthodox brahmins break their fast begun on the previous day (*ekadasi*, the eleventh day).

Page 18

bund: embanked causeway.

Page 19

twice-born: *dvija*, the epithet applies not only to brahmins and the other two upper-castes (*kshatriya* 'warrior', *vaisya* 'tradesman') but also to birds, snakes, various grains, and to teeth, etc.—anything that may be said to have two births (e.g. birds and snakes are born as eggs and reborn from them). Snakes are considered sacred and therefore should be cremated ceremoniously.

Hedonist School: the Charvaka School, materialists and hedonist philosophers, who believed in the slogan quoted—equivalent to 'Enjoy yourself, even if it's on borrowed money'.

ghee: clarified butter.

decadent age: *kali*, the present age, the last and the most decadent of the four ages.

permanent perfume: a classic precedent for a sage lusting after a low-caste woman. Sage Parashara took Matsyagandhi ('the fish-scented woman') on the river as she rowed him across—and blessed her body with a perennial fragrance.

aposhana: cf. note on p. 3.

Achari: a vulgar disrespectful form of Acharya. In Acharya-re '-re' is a respectful vocative suffix. Naranappa plays with both forms here.

Kalidasa's heroine Shakuntala: Kalidasa, the great Sanskrit poet and dramatist (fifth century?). His most celebrated heroine is Shakuntala.

Hari: another name of Narayana or Vishnu.

Ash Demon: *Bhasmasura* obtained from Shiva a boon—that he could burn to cinders anyone on whose head he placed his hands. As soon as he received the boon, he wished to test it on Shiva himself who ran to Vishnu for rescue. Vishnu assumed the form of a seductive woman, and enticed Bhasmasura to learn Indian dancing. One of the dance postures required him to place his palm on his own head, which sent the gullible demon up in flames.

raised verandah: *jagali*, pyol.

Vedanta: 'the end of the Vedas', or the essential creed, expounded by three great Hindu philosophers, Shankara, Ramanuja, and Madhva.

rule for emergencies: *apaddharma,* a relaxation of ethical or other rules (dharma) during an emergency.

Page 31

Yakshagana: a popular dance-drama of South Kannada country on classical themes.

Page 33

Kuchela: a poor thin brahmin, who was a devotee and a friend of Lord Krishna.

Page 34

Trivikrama: one of the ten incarnations of Vishnu: Vishnu appears as a dwarf (*Vamana*) to demon-king Bali and asks only for a small gift of land, measured by three paces of his small feet, which Bali unwittingly grants him, whereupon the dwarf grows to cosmic proportions (*Trivikrama*) and measures all of earth with one step, all the heavens with another, and with his third step pushes the awe-struck but enlightened demon Bali into the nether world.

Page 37

Nine Essences: *rasa*, 'flavour, essence', a central concept in Indian aesthetics. The business of art is to compose, make, evoke, present, etc. one or more *rasas* in the listener, reader, etc. The feelings of real life are *bhavas*, the raw material; the work of art composes, refines, structures, generalizes, etc. these into *rasas*. There are, traditionally, nine *rasas*.

Page 38

Menaka, Vishvamitra: cf. note on p. 98.

Page 44

ever-auspicious, daily-wedded: *nitya-sumangali*, etc., traditional (and often ironic) description of prostitutes.

Page 46

Draupadi: in the epic *Mahabharata*, Draupadi, wife of the five Pandava brothers, is wagered and lost to their rivals and cousins, the Kauravas, in a dice game. One of the Kaurava brothers drags her into court by her sari. She cries out to Lord Krishna for help, who miraculously makes the sari endless—so the molester finds it impossible to disrobe her. On other occasions, too, Draupadi prays to Krishna for help, never in vain—a common theme in mythological plays.

Page 48

Indra, Yama, Varuna: Vedic gods. Indra: God of Heaven, the Rain God; Yama: God of Death; Varuna: God of the Seas.

Page 51

sacred designs: *rangavalli, rangoli*, auspicious and ornamental designs drawn with various coloured powders on the floor, in front of a house or an idol.

gain-O gain: in measuring numbers one and seven are taboo. One is called 'gain' (*labha*), and seven 'one more'.

Page 55

food taboos (for brahmins): Dasacharya, a Madhva, would be breaking a taboo and would lose ritual status by eating cooked food in a Smarta house. For Madhva and Smarta, cf. note on p. 5.

Page 58

Sitavva: *avva* or 'mother' is a respectful suffix added to women's names by servants, etc. So Sitadevi is called Sitavva here.

Page 60

flaming camphor: *mangalarati*, the lamp-service in a temple, when gongs and drums are beaten, conches blown; flowers, fruits and flaming camphor are offered to the deity's image.

Page 62

epic war: in the epic *Ramayana*, Maruti, or Hanumana, the monkey-devotee of Rama, carried a whole mountain on which grew life-giving herbal plants which alone could save Lakshmana (Rama's brother) who had received a death-wound. In Maruti's temples, the monkey-god is often represented with a mountain on the palm of his hand.

Page 64

amma: an intimate form of address for one's mother, like mom, mummy, etc., in English.

Page 67

constellation of the Seven Sages: the constellation Ursa Major, the Big Dipper. The seven stars are supposed to be seven sages.

Page 69

farmers' section: *keri*, usually any exclusive street or section where the lower castes (farmers, etc.) live; the non-brahmin counterpart of the brahmin *agrahara*.

Page 71

Hirannayya: once a famous actor on the Kannada stage.

Page 72

Vamana, Trivikrama: cf. note on p. 34.

Page 73

Sadarame, Shakuntale: Kannada names of heroines in popular plays; cf. note on p. 25.

Page 74

life-breaths: *prana*, the soul (as opposed to the body), vital power. Tradition lists five such vital 'breaths'.

Page 75

baby monkey: probably a reference to the way of the Monkey, or *markatanyaya*. The soul has two possible kinds of relations with the lord: (a) like a baby monkey (*markata*) he may hold on to the mother-monkey as she goes about her business, indifferent to the little dependent; (b) like a kitten (*marjara*) he may do nothing, letting the mother-cat pick him up and move him where she will. (a) is the analogue of the way of Works, and (*b*) of the way of Faith (and surrender to God's grace).

Page 76

mantras: the *gayatri* mantra, a Vedic prayer/hymn, repeated by every brahmin at his morning and evening devotions; also chanted thousands of times to accumulate merit.

Goodness: *sattvika, rajasika, tamasika*, 'Men of Goodness, Energy, or Darkness' (Zaehner's tr.). There are three constituents or 'strands' (*guna*) in all natural beings: *sattva* (goodness), *rajas* (passion, energy), *tamas* (darkness). Human beings differ according to the predominance of one or the other. For a clear text, cf. *The Bhagavadgita* 8.40: 'There is no existent thing in heaven or earth nor yet among the gods which is or ever could be free from these three constituents from Nature sprung'. References to *gunas* are translated here by 'Good' nature, 'Energy' etc. with capitals.

Page 77

Urvashi: a celestial nymph (*apsara*). The sight of her beauty is said to have caused the generation of certain sages. She was also cursed by the gods to live upon the earth, and became the love of Pururavas. Kalidasa (cf. note on p. 25) wrote a play about their love. Like the myth of Parashara earlier, here is another myth connecting human and divine, beauty and sanctity, erotic and ascetic,—sharpening one of the central themes of this novel.

Page 81

counter-clockwise: ritually speaking, clockwise (moving to the right) circumambulations (of an idol, a brahmin, a holy place, etc.) are auspicious, counter-clockwise movements are not.

155

Matsyagandhi: the fish-scented woman, cf. note on p. 23.

five-fold breath of life: cf. note on p. 74.

wet dhotis: after a cremation, the brahmins have to bathe and wash their clothes. *Dhotis* are unstitched pieces of cloth worn by men wrapped round the waist.

remains of the body: the remains after a cremation, the ashes, bones, etc. are immersed in a running stream.

Mari: the dark goddess of death, plague, etc.; often a term of abuse.

dualities: *dvandvas*, like pain/pleasure, love/hate, are to be transcended. cf. *The Bhagavadgita*, 2.45.

Trishanku: a king who engaged Sage Vishvamitra (cf. below) to send him to heaven against the will of the King of Heaven, Indra. Vishvamitra rocketed him heavenwards with his spiritual power, but Indra didn't accept him. So Trishanku hung between two worlds and became the symbol for all those who hang similarly.

Vyasa: the sage and compiler of the epic *Mahabharata* was the offspring of an illicit union between the fisherwoman Matsyagandhi and Sage Parashara.

Vishvamitra: a king turned sage, often given to passions of lust, pride and rage; was frequently tempted and lost his spiritual earnings. A celestial nymph, Menaka, was once sent to tempt him away from his penances which imperilled Indra, the Rain-God.

Jayadeva's Song about Krishna: *Gitagovinda*, Jayadeva's celebrated (12th century) religious/erotic poem about Krishna and his loves. The Sanskrit line quoted runs as follows: *Lalitalavangalataparishilana-komalamalayasamire*.

Malera: a community (as suggested later) rather low in others' esteem, allegedly the offspring of brahmins and their mistresses, out of wedlock.

Page 102
   bidi: small Indian cigarette, tobacco rolled in dried leaves.

Page 103
   Tayinadu: a Kannada newspaper, well known a few decades ago.
Tayinadu means 'Motherland'. The novelist identifies the time of the
novel by such references.

Page 106
   Raghavendra: another name of Rama, 'king of the dynasty of Raghus',
specially worshipped by Madhvas of this region.

Page 115
   dose: 'a holed, i.e. spongy cake of rice-flour, pulses, etc. baked on a
potsherd or ironplate' (Kittel).

Page 115
   low seat: *mane*, a low wooden seat.

Page 118
   keri: cf. note on p. 69.

Page 119
   kali: cf. note on p. 22.

Page 121
   monism, advaita: cf. note on p. 5.
   That art Thou: *tattvamasi*, the famous monistic formula.

Page 124
   darshan: the sight of a holy object, image, deity or person—such a
glimpse is participatory, rewarding.

Page 126
   ek ana: 'one anna' (anna being a small coin, a nickel, now obsolete) in
Urdu or Hindustani. Such references mark the story as non-contem-
porary, strengthening the effect of an allegory in a densely realistic
setting.

Page 129
   Bhimasena: the second of the Pandava brothers, known for his
strength, size and appetite. cf. note on p. 16.

Page 133
   Sahukar: 'the rich man', here obviously a rich local donor.

Page 135
   Southern breezes . . . clove: line from *Gitagovinda*, cf. note on p. 99.

Page 141

'*Just as a work . . . prescribed rite*': Parashara, quoted by P. V. Kane, *History of Dharmashastra*, Volume II, Part I (Poona, 1941), pp. 189–90.

'*perpetually deferred reply*': Roland Barthes, on Balzac's *Sarrasine*, in *S/Z*, tr. Richard Miller (New York, 1974), p. 84.

Page 142

rite de passage: see Arnold van Gennep, *Rites of Passage* (London, 1960; first published 1908). For further explorations of the 'liminal', see Victor Turner, *The Ritual Process* (Chicago, 1969).

Page 143

the god-heretic: cf. Wendy O'Flaherty's *Asceticism and Eroticism in the Mythology of Siva* (London, 1973).

Page 147

Samskara *as a novel of decadent Hinduism*: M. G. Krishnamurti, *Adhunika Bharatiya Sahitya* (1970). Here, and elsewhere in these pages, I am indebted to G. H. Nayak's and S. Nagarajan's articles in *Sakshi 11* (1971), and to M. G. Krishnamurti's essay.